Books from Life Is Amazing with

Fiction
Portsmouth Fairy Tales for Grown-Ups (anthology)
Day of the Dead (anthology)
By Celia's Arbour, A Tale of Portsmouth Town
(by Walter Besant and James Rice)
Dark City (anthology)

Non-Fiction
Ten Years In A Portsmouth Slum
(by Robert Dolling)
The History of Portsmouth
(by Lake Allen)
Recollections of John Pounds
(by Henry Hawkes)

Humour / Novelty
A Pompey Person's Guide to Everything Great About
Southampton
Southampton Person's Guide to Everything Great About
Portsmouth

With all best wishes!

THE SNOW WITCH

Matt Wingett

Life Is Amazing

A Life Is Amazing Paperback

The Snow Witch

First published 2017 by Life Is Amazing
ISBN: 978-0-9956394-5-4
First Edition

Part 1

THE shop doorway was the best shelter she could find.

She draws on a cigarette and raises her eyes to the dull morning sky, where sparse flakes are falling. Her face is a delta of narrow chin and wideset eyes, her skin white beneath her long black hair. Pulling the pale fabric of her fur-edged coat close around her, she stamps in her boots.

She hitched into town last night and was caught seeking shelter by a blizzard that exploded from nowhere. She won't move on again. *Not when it's this bad,* she thinks, sniffing the air and smelling another storm coming, an instinct she learned somewhere a long way away. She stretches and shivers and feels the ache in her twenty-nine-year-old limbs, then clamps the cigarette between her teeth, stuffs her sleeping bag into her rucksack and tightens the straps with jerking movements.

What now? she asks herself, looking around. She considers a small black case on the floor by the rucksack, inhales, exhales, shrugs.

Get some cash, buy food, and, finally, a ticket, she talks to herself in her head. *As soon as I can – get away.*

This, then, is a plan.

She flicks the cigarette butt and screws it into the ground with her sole. Selecting a pitch beside a shop – *Here's as good as anywhere* – with a gentle *knock* and *click*, she leans over her case and opens it.

A violin.

The familiar weight and curve of the neck presses her palm as her audience arrives: pale shopkeepers, fluorescent council men, early-morning shoppers, red-flushed kids excited by snowfall.

Fresh, bright, sad: sensual notes dip and turn in the winter light. The melody is alien. Rich. It conjures foreign terrain, snowclad peaks, a stream, the resin scent of mountain pines.

Two fat boys gawp, their hearts lifting. A young man behind thick glasses stops in his tracks, his mouth agape in the chill air. An elderly woman slides on the ice with a deftness that speaks the delight she felt before age embrittled her bones.

The magic in the music works, like it always works. Even the snow holds off and more people come by, entranced by her melodies. Soon, the musician scoops coins from her case and wolfs hot pastries and steaming coffee before resuming, playing on through the day. When she rests in the darkening afternoon, snow begins to fall again, piling whiteness on whiteness, laying a carpet of crystal beneath her feet.

When she finishes, she glances over her shoulder to check she is not being followed, and goes.

*

Stranded by weather and lack of money, she stays for a day, and then another. A hunger for company grows in her and the pubs draw her in.

She has a habit when she first enters a pub: she stands in the doorway and waits with her head tilted. Standing tall, perfectly still, case-over-shoulder, she looks as if she is sensing the mood of the room. Only once she is satisfied it is safe to enter does she step in.

One afternoon, in *The Barleymow*, a local sees the case and asks her if she "plays that thing". She rests her chin upon the violin and once again trills magic into the air.

One evening, in *The King Street* which stands on a cobbled corner she joins the Irish Session and weaves sumptuous harmonies through their jigs and reels.

Then, in *The Tavern* at the far end of the long beach fronting the city onto the south sea, she joins a late-night jam.

Here, one pair of eyes in particular scrutinises her. She feels them burn her.

When she leaves, she knows the watcher will follow her into a night that has grown so late it is early. *These men are so predictable,* she thinks. She has noted him and will dispense with him.

So it is that he tracks her compacted steps for a hundred metres from the pub door, then double-takes when he sees the trail end at the kerb, with nothing beyond but ice and snow.

For her part, moving out of sight, she pictures him in her mind's eye and smiles to herself.

This is her habit. She will not be followed.

*

The man swaying at the intersection between two terraced streets is Riley.

He stands two metres tall, in a long leather coat and black, wide-brimmed hat. Beneath it, black curls writhe into a thick beard that frames a strong face with full, sensual lips.

"Fuck," a hot syllable in the air.

Something about her... He cocks his head, as if straining to hear an unclear call from his past crackling with the static of years. Whatever that message is, he wishes he could go back to hear it.

Maybe I can, he thinks, stumbling down the street, half-drunk, half-stoned.

*

Riley.

Riley.

Everyone who has ever played music in a pub knows him. They know the way the twenty-eight-year-old swaggers in at open mic sessions and, looming over the MC, takes charge. Or how, in jam sessions he arrives with his own amplification to drown his rivals in sound.

He has his following. Kids in the city's long lines of concrete flats and post-war estates pop his pills. Glistening addicts, strung out and desperate, call his number in their long dark nights. *Their taut skin in the lamplight, drawn in on themselves, shaking.* He pictures their interrelation. Him: their medic, their doctor, their salvation. Them: desperate for white powder.

His head is dull darkness as he walks the whited streets. He snorted the last of his own white powder hours before and life now weighs on him. *Snow. Fucking snow,* he eyes the flakes whirling in lamplight and selects a street parallel with the sea.

Passing a deep-buried pitch-and-putt by the seafront, the come-down takes hold, creating a wave of self-pity and world-directed rage.

Early January, winter nights – so fucking long.

He imagines himself pushed up close to that foreign fiddler's body, his drink-magnified sense of slight looping toward rage. *What is she? Foreign? A gyppo maybe? Anyway, shouldn't be so fucking ignorant.*

And she *was* ignorant.

The whole night he was attentive, asking where she learned to play so well – commenting on *the delicacy of her touch, the way she chooses her notes.*

He learned that stuff from his dad. He hoiks a phlegm in the snow. *As if I gave a shit about her playing.*

Perhaps she knew. She blanked him continually – a provocation in itself – dropping her bow when he tried to take charge of the ring of jamming musicians.

She seized her opportunity when a drunk girl with a fox tattoo draped herself over him. *A gust of cold air, door closing, smoked-glass windows, silhouette flitting on glass.*

By the time he had thrown off the kid and pulled on his hat and coat, the street was devoid of movement. And then...

Tracks leading nowhere. What happened there?

He dismisses it.

Stuck-up gyppo bitch.

He arrives at a white expanse, the heads of black railings jut from the snow; nearby, a stunted litter bin: a dwarf sentry in white-domed helmet. In the middle distance, a ring of plastic swans – a lake, indistinct, as are the roads and garden edges around it.

Here he is: *back in time;* back here at the lake across from his mother's house.

On the water's surface he feels the *crunch* of snow, and the *crack* and *boom* as the ice sheet tenses. He heads with purpose to the plastic pedalos, relics of the '60s with swan necks and funny-grotesque faces. He climbs on and sprawls across them, letting his head go back, snowflakes melting on his upturned face and delivering remembrance:

From the window of my mother's house; kids playing; sparkling water. The old man in his flat cap palming coins and notes in return for twenty shimmering minutes; he's watching for me coz of that time I took a boat. To go where?

He sees himself: a directionless impulse surrounded by concrete banks; no escape except if that plastic swan should stretch its wings and fly. *No fucking chance.*

There is something he wants to remember. But now he is here, in the magic circle of his childhood, the voices and pictures crowd in, making it impossible to see straight.

There was a time, a long way back. A time. Before... all this shit.

Riley shudders, lifts his head abruptly and props himself on his elbows, staring ahead. He absorbs the winter night, the lines of bulbs along the resort's seafront glowing in reds, yellows and blues, coloured globes of snow-filled air. He can hear the sea you can always hear on the front, can smell saltwater in iced air. *The sea. The black, black sea...*

A calm sinks through him until it reaches the centre of his being, where it shatters. He senses weakness. On instinct, he climbs off the swan onto the ice, turns and grips its long neck, pulling hard. The fibreglass holds a while and he doubles his effort, jerking it over and over with all his weight till it cracks off with a sputtering wrench and he throws it into the snow.

He imagines the old-man-of-the-pedalos lying there. Then he sees the neck's gentle line and thinks again of the fiddle player, and laughs.

Snow is falling thick and fast, obscuring the line of the white pier in the half distance, dropping on his eyes like ashes, or kisses, or dust.

Cold.

He shivers toward a parade of run-down shops. *3 a.m.* He bangs a door with the flat of his hand and shouts *VEE!* – the word erupting in a syllable of steam.

A mother-of-two in her mid-twenties with worn-through slippers and a cheap dressing gown clutched at the neck answers the door. *Weary. Shivering. Resigned.* He senses her kids staring from the top of the stairs, stumbles in, swears, demands coffee. She goes to make it, hearing him stomp upstairs, crashing onto her bed, his energy drained by cold and cocaine.

She brings the mug, stands by the bed and looks down with more resignation, noticing the clothes he is wearing dripping melted dirt over her sheets.

He can be good, she tells herself. *He can be great.*

She takes the cup away and heads downstairs. The sofa awaits. And sleep.

*

Sleep.

The city sleeps, contracted in the cold to a singularity of stone. An island city, surrounded by tides flooding from the south, running up its eastern side, swelling the creek that orphans it from the mainland, swirling through its western harbour where it welcomes boats disgorging shivering holidaymakers and businesspeople and soldiers and home-comers and refugees.

A city just 5 miles long, with tight furrows in which were planted, in the last century-and-a half, rows of terraced housing hunched in lines, braced against the gushing sea gale. Long before they grew, to the south of the island, a few bleak, isolated cottages stood beside a long, muddy beach. Within a few decades, the health-giving sea attracted a rash of tall villas set back from the shore, separated from the ever-moving water by a desolate common. Upon it, from time to time, troops marshalled under white canvas bell tents between furze bushes near a small fortress garrisoned with redcoats. Later, as the salubrious saline's effects grew fashionable, bathing machines rolled in, a pier sprouted, beach huts, ice-cream stands, and, in the by-now obsolete heart of the lonely fortress, a model village. Later too, the great morass where the island's river waters pooled, was channelled into a manmade lake – and so the plastic swans were trucked in, to move upon the face of the water.

Beyond this southern leisure resort, the real business of the island unfolded in the west. How often had marshalled troops marched from the common in drilled ranks to the dockyard and embarked on ships? To this day, beyond the seaside resort and the old town that stretches along a spit of land to a tiny, hook-shaped harbour, ferries and freighters and warships wallow in giant docks, waiting to transport people, and goods, and death.

All that can be found on the city's western edge: at the dockyard, at the container quay, at the ferryport.

*

At the ferryport, newcomers are disembarking,

On the shore, they gaze up into the whirling white, then hurry for warmth and hotels or onward journeys.

One among them is different from the rest. Perhaps the city's more sensitive dreamers feel his presence as he grounds himself on the tarmac. *A slim figure, green eyes, animal-fluid movements.*

Outside the terminal, he bares his white teeth and tastes the snow on his tongue, separating the air's interwoven spoors. Satisfied, he nods to himself, then slips into the shadows where the island's dreams live.

For a moment, a cold breath over the city frets the sleepers under their covers. Some turn, blow a shadow across the room, then slip back into unconsciousness, the islands of their beds washed by a turbulent ocean of dreams.

*

Dreams.

In Vee's house the dreams have descended upon each sleeper with their own particular horror: night visitors pinning the dreamers to their beds, filling their helpless heads. The fat boys cannot shake their grip. One fights a giant snake in a jungle made of sticks of rock; the other dreams of a bicycle that flies over their home and lifts him to fresh heights above the clouds. Upwards and upwards until the Earth itself is a tiny speck on which he gazes, seeing the people below walking to keep it turning, walking onwards forever, some dying on the way, but others newborn stumbling up from the ground to keep it turning, turning, turning. He loses his balance and tumbles downward, ricocheting from the stars like the metal ball in a pinball machine, until he is walking on the ground, turning the ball of the Earth beneath his feet, on an eternal round.

Vee dreams her recurring dream. She is walking on a sandy beach, the air around her warm and gentle. Somewhere in the distance, a black dog is eating something. She goes toward it, terrified of what she will find, and sees a painting of her parents that she made when she was a child, being devoured. The dog sees her and steps forward baring its teeth.

Riley dreams of pigs. Snuffling little pigs who run loose over the ground, eating everything they can. A senseless dream of shouts and snuffles, snouts and shuffles and squeals of delight which revolve in his head and have no shape, but make only noise, growing ever more real and pulsing in time with the throbbing of his drug-sapped brain.

*

He is woken by Vee's two boys playing on the stairs. His head a blacksmith's anvil, his throat a dry gully. He snaps open his bloodshot eyes and shouts down from the bedroom.

"Shut the fuck up!"

There is silence for a few minutes, until the kids drop a plastic toy car as the fear wears off.

"Shut the fuck up or I swear I will drown you."

The idea appeals to him now, catching his imagination with grim amusement, and he stands and saunters to the top of the stairs.

Two overweight boys, terrified, looking up. He glares at them, playing the villain to himself, enjoying the wideness of their eyes and the paling of their fat faces.

"Listen, listen," he speaks quietly in deference to his headache. The boys strain to hear. "Carry on like that, here's my promise. I'll tie you up in a sack and drop you in the sea." He pauses. *"The sea. The black, black sea,"* he inhales deep, then exhales through vibrating lips that flap together. Shaking his head: "Nasty way to go."

His gaze is distant for a second. Then he straightens, glares down at them. He laughs as he pictures himself standing over them. He savours these flashes of power. A moment of stillness when his impulses find a focus. He considers these *fat little piggies.*

"I'm hungry, boys," he slaps his hands together and rubs the palms and licks his lips. "So, then. What do you do..?"

He glares the question. The boys fix him silently with their eyes, alert for a sudden move. Their rigid attention pleases him:

"Piggies, cook the bacon. How I like it. Don't overdo it. - *Well, go on!"*

He raises a dismissive arm; enough to send them scrabbling into the kitchen. A few minutes later, he can hear the sound of pots and pans. He laughs: a snapshot of their frightened faces in his mind. *A picture*, he chuckles to himself. *What a picture.*

He gazes through the window at the white, white snow on the backs of the houses and a memory takes hold of him. *That gyppo girl. Where is she?*

*

Donitza Kravitch is drinking coffee not 400 metres from where Riley is obsessing about her, the vapour rising and expanding across her face creating alert relaxation. There is a smell of sponge cake pervading the room with a soft vanilla butteriness that dispels the thought of the snow outside. A woman's voice is humming in another room, intoning *Good Day Sunshine* in a contented way, accompanied by the bustling hiss of aerosol polish applied to every shiny surface.

Donitza smiles for a moment at the noise. Everything here is so normal. So everyday. From the funny squat powder-blue ceramic figurine of a lady in a crinoline and a grey wig, frozen forever in a look of elegant amusement at the world, to the old black-and-white photograph of a man in his thirties in a smart suit, smiling into the camera with an expression of cheeky bravado, eternally captured. The fact is, the room speaks of a life and Donitza is grateful to it.

She is grateful to the collection of thimbles in a mounted wooden box on the wall, divided into square pigeonholes, each big enough to hold a thumbguard. She is grateful to the way the water gurgles from the old gas boiler, and to the dustless warmth offered by the 1970s British Government to its people in the form of gas central heating. She is grateful for coffee, and for little bread rolls from the Co-op that taste of nothing in particular, which the old lady chooses in preference to *that foreign stuff - no offence dear -* that she can't quite pronounce, but are called *croissants*.

But most of all, she is grateful to Celia. Dear, dear Celia who smiled at her on that first day when she walked by her as she played, and then slid playfully on the ice, then later brought her a slice of cake as the day darkened, and asked her where she was staying. When the strange slim Eastern European girl shrugged and told her she didn't know, she invited her into her home, telling her with a carefree voice:

"I have a spare bed. And the house is warm. Very warm and cosy, and too big for me on my own."

In fact, the house is not very big. One of many tight terraces on the south east side of the island, which huddle in neat Victorian staves, codaed by shingle at the sea end. They are in an area described by estate agents as *the village* to add a veneer of class. This little place, it is big enough after all. For now it is a home.

A home. Donitza thinks the words dispassionately, turning the noun over in her mind and approaching it carefully, from an oblique direction, peering at it distrustfully. It is a word that is not only alien to her for the strange soft language the English speak, but for the meaning it conveys. For her, when she thinks of this word she thinks of a vast, terrible whiteness, like frost on a window, obscuring the view inside. Sometimes she imagines herself reaching out a hand to clear that window, but feels sudden weakness, and she shrinks away. She lives only now, making no connections, waking no memories. The past, that is where the emotion is, and she will not go there to meet it, but forever moves forward to escape it.

She shakes herself, and looks up to see Celia eyeing her from the doorway, holding a yellow duster in her Marigolded hands.

"You all right dear?" she asks, knowing with her woman's knowledge that she is not. And knowing too, with her woman's knowledge that she will not get an honest answer.

"Yes, I am fine, Celia," the Eastern European girl answers. "Fine, fine." She pulls her arms in around her, seeming to hug her ribs in a defensive manoeuvre. Then she reaches for her cigarette, inhales and throws her head back as she allows the smoke to go down deep, feeling for a moment its warmth reach inside her and quicken her heart.

"That'll kill you sooner than needs be," Celia says. "Much too soon."

To her shrug she adds: "What will you do today?"

"I will play," Donitza replies after a few seconds as she recognises the ritual they have fallen into. "Just like every other day."

"But it's freezing out there. Not seen it like this for years. Unnatural cold – and you're out there in it. Freezing," says Celia, a look of heartbreak at this poor girl going out in the snow, just as she has done since she moved in.

Donitza shrugs again and looks at the burning end of her cigarette. She has played in worse weather and worse places. This is how she lives.

*

In the pedestrian precinct the snow has come down so thick the council men have nearly given up clearing the streets. But there are still people around, and Donitza takes out her violin from its case and begins to bow it.

It's a warming melody, and people gather round her to thaw their souls. There is one in the crowd she saw before on that first day, a quiet young man who smiles – shy and wan – in thick glasses. She notices him stay, shivering, as others go by.

It is a week since she arrived here, and she is becoming known, she realises, with a prickle of discomfort. People are giving her nods, and familiar smiles – friendly frowns that say she must be mad to be out playing in this. Then there are the eyes of the shy man swimming behind their glasses, who looks at her palely, that don't have a look of concern, but something else. Admiration. Awe, even.

Her fingers are freezing as she plays, making the warmth inside her burn more hotly. They may all think she's crazy to carry on the way she does, but the reality is she has to. It was something her mother said to her, many years ago – part of the tradition of her life. Her playing sends away the oppressive blankness that hovers over her heart and on her shoulders and fills the air she breathes; it brings her only to the present, and dispels whatever presses forward on the other side of the whiteness.

Today, however, as she plays, Donitza's mind begins to wander backwards, despite her efforts to stay on the flux of notes she creates. The images in her mind fascinate her and repel her as she becomes aware of her memories moving before her. Something the old lady Celia did this morning, a tiny thing, has woken creatures she wishes had stayed asleep.

It was a simple action when she brought her a cup of coffee. Three times she cleared her throat, then walked in without any sense of boundary, as if she were her mother, and, with the cup stabilised skilfully in her hand, pulled back the curtains with a single movement.

Her silhouette! Emerging from the whiteness of her memory an image came back to Donitza of her past, and she numbly stared. That shape in the window. A simple movement, laden with memories.

Celia had turned toward her, cup in hand, and placed it on her bed, oblivious to the storm she had sparked.

Her eyes were filled with her own remembered pleasure. Yes, she had pulled back the curtains, but not for Donitza.

"Here's your drink, Janey," she said as she leaned beside her bed. "So nice to have you home again."

Then she placed her old woman's hand on the younger woman's forehead. "Lovely to have you here." Absently she stroked her hair, then straightened with a joyous smile and left the room with an almost-skip.

Later in the morning, in the cold kitchen of the tidy house, Donitza was seated at a small blue formica-topped table when she asked Celia, standing by the sink. "Who is Janey?"

Celia stared at her with a prickle of superstitious horror. "How do you know about Janey?" she asked sharply. Then she demanded with more force: "HOW DO YOU KNOW ABOUT JANEY?"

Donitza was startled by the flash of anger, but then Celia's emotions turned in on themselves and she came over to sit beside the young woman, putting her wrinkled hand over Donitza's.

"Janey," she sighed after a while, her exhalation materialising a breathghost in the morning light. "Now, now dear. Did I mention Janey?" She gave her a look. "All in good time."

Now, in the present moment, playing in the precinct, Donitza feels a tear swell in her eye – an emotion she is not used to, and notices she is playing a long sad melody from her childhood. All these feelings from a single action.

The window of remembrance unfrosted; she looks again and despite herself peers through to relive a scene from her past –

Her mother is folding shut a paper packet and singing in a

focussed way. She seals the tiny packet with a dab of glue then writes upon it. Next, she lifts something from the table and turns to her daughter.

"What is this lady called?" she asks with a delicate and precise act of checking, holding a stalk before her. Donitza can feel the struggle in her mind, but also the way her uncertainty is smoothed by her mother's kindly look, the encouraging tone, the gentle verification of the knowledge she has imparted, unique to her, that will stand her in good stead in years to come.

"That is Aconite mother," she says, proudly, enjoying the game.

"Good," she nods, wisely. "And how else is she invoked?"

"As the bane of wolf, of leopard and of woman. She is also conjured as the hood of monk and cap of the devil."

"And what planet rules her?"

"Saturn, mother. Saturn... is that right?"

"That's right, my Flower, and what are her virtues?"

The girl takes a breath. "She is home to a soul who bars the doorway to poison. A decoction of her root makes a bath to wash a body bitten by venomous animals." She pauses, seeing her mother's approval, and goes on. "And there is a dust in her flower that, with particular incantations, is baleful to the sight, irritating and ultimately stealing the soul from the eyes."

"Good. Very good. Who is the mother of Mistress Aconita?"

"Isis, of the Nile, for her daughter requires damp but well-drained soils. Her father is Atlas, and like her father, Aconita also loves the mountains. Wet, high and cold – these are the houses her parents made for her."

Her mother smiles with deep satisfaction, picking another cut stalk from the table and holding it before her. "Now this one..."

But the girl sits back away from her. "Mother, can we stop a while? I am tired and my head is so very full. I can see flowers sprouting out of my own eyes!"

Her mother looks at her seriously for a moment, then seeing the disgruntled look on her face, laughs loudly. "Yes, my Sparrow. You can rest from this. But here," she grows serious again and lifts the violin from the table. "Make this sing me a tune – one of the songs I have taught you. The melody works its way into the herbs."

"Can I not rest, Mama? Please?"

But her mother's attention is elsewhere. She raises a quietening hand and walks to the window, head cocked, drawing the curtain quickly back in that distinctive way of hers, a silhouette at the window, looking out with intense eyes at the mountain firs, the snow heavy on them.

She stands in silence for a moment until Donitza makes to move from her chair.

"Shh. Did you hear something?"

Donitza sighs. "No, I didn't hear anything," she says, bored with that question. How many times has that drama been rehearsed? She props her head on her delicate fist, sinking her seven-year-old's cheek upon it, and exhales a sigh.

Her mother continues to peer through the window, breathing in shallow breaths, searching intensely the eaves of the trees for signs of disturbance. A wolf is skirting the shade at their edge, the whites and greys of its coat stand out briefly and then are lost again.

After a moment she comes back to the table. "We must be ready," she says. "Bad men are coming. I don't know when. But we must be ready."

She leans and strokes the girl's dark hair for a moment, gazing into her daughter's eyes with an earnest look. "You will need to be brave my Sparrow. Do you understand?"

Donitza feels an intense weight in her mother's stare and is not sure what to say. Then her mother breaks the spell by handing her the violin.

"We are different from the others here. Their fight will not be ours."

"How mother? How are we different?"

Her mother pauses, gently biting her lower lip as she considers. "Play. Always play," she says. "It will make the magic stronger."

The memory fades as the day darkens, tilting afternoon into evening. The lights in the shops are filling the air with blocks of light – squares and trapezoids that lie on the snow as if discarded by a careless workman.

She plays on, noticing the young man in the glasses turn away at last, though he has stared and stared for what must be an hour. His face is tinged with blue, she thinks as she sees him dart toward the warmth of a shop, crossing the pools of light gathered on the snow.

She tries to surrender herself to the flux of notes around her, to step into the stream of the present as it flies from her violin. But today her memory has been awakened and will not let her live in the now. One shape cast on the snow is the exact shape she saw years before, flat on the grass. She cannot help herself. As she plays, she remembers again – pulled backward by the old images. The present is gone –

She wakes from deep sleep to a commotion echoing through the night. "Quick!" her mother shouts to her. "Quickly now!"

She drags herself from bed, grabbing her boots and hopping from the room as she struggles to pull them on, while her mother hefts a stick and runs to the blackshrouded garden. It is summer, the night air rich with the scents of herbs and the gentle pulse of crickets. In the soft warm darkness, the source of the commotion stands to the left, low and dark, a parallelogram of light cast toward it from the doorway. A chorus of panic hymning in the darkness.

"Out! Get out!" her mother shouts at the shed that has exploded with the violent horror inside. "Out!" She dances around it, striking its wooden sides with the stick; three mighty cracks. With her other hand she grasps the handle.

The sound in the shed has died down by the time she wrenches the door open. In the night shadow, Donitza sees a low, pointed shape slide between her mother's feet, moving with deadly speed and purpose. It looks back, its eyes glinting green in the low light and gazes at Donitza for two long seconds.

Her mother hurls her stick. "Gaah! Yaah! Go on!"

The shape dissolves into the darkness.

Her mother steps inside and there is silence for a few seconds, then a curse. She steps out, locks up, tight-lipped and comes back to the cottage, muttering under her breath.

"Fox," she says. "Damned fox. That one has a mind of his own."

She looks at Donitza with narrowed eyes. The girl feels like she will die under that glare.

The following morning Donitza blinks in at the roosts where the hens had been sleeping. Spatters of blood dot the walls and dark stains mark the boards at her feet. White, brown and black feathers are trapped in blackening blood. Bodies are scattered in their roosts, or hanging over the edges, some with a gaping hole in their throats or lolling broken-necked with their heads at improbable angles; others, completely untouched, are dead of fright. Donitza gawps around with heart in mouth as she envisions the destructive force that hurricaned through that tiny room.

Her mother directs her to gather the carcasses. They are stiffening with rigor mortis. Handling their cold solidity, Donitza begins to feel an ache behind her eyes, and a hot throb tightening in her throat. She feels sick. Her mother turns and asks in a measured tone.

"Did you lock the door yesterday?"

Donitza gulps, a stone in her stomach growing heavier, plummeting through her body.

"I – ," she stops as the image flits before her. Joyously skipping out, breaking into a carefree run, gleefully shooing the hens into the coop, then throwing the latch distractedly as she laughs about the story she has just been told.

The story is of two men. She has heard it before – but not like this.

It is told this way: One man died and now has the power to breathe life into the dead. His enemy is the Red Man. These two – the Red Man and the Dead Man play some kind of game to gather the dead to themselves. There are sets of rules as to who receives whom.

Her mother had explained it all with a deadpan face, which made Donitza giggle all the more. The whole story looked at this way was preposterous! By the end of it, as her mother finished off with, "And that, they believe, is the meaning of their lives," Donitza had collapsed in a heap on the floor. Ridiculous!

After a while, her mother had said: "Now, child, go and close the shed."

Afterwards, Donitza had stood outside, looking down at the valley in the evening light. Her mother had stood beside her and pointed at the church tower and minaret. "Masculine and feminine in form," the matriarch said. "I wonder if they can see the realities beneath their faiths? – But of course they can't!"

What with her laughter and her puzzlement at her mother's implied meanings, little wonder she had thrown the latch hastily. Did she secure it? She can't remember. It was the opening a fox as red as blood needed to steal in from the darkness.

"I –," she says again, tears running down her face. "I thought I had, Mama, I thought –" and then she stops as a wracking sob comes up from deep in her belly. It all rests on her.

Her mother looks at her, devoid of pity as she lifts another carcass.

"These are our responsibilities," she says quietly. "To guard our brood. To protect. To make safe. That is the covenant between us and the creatures we live with. Last night you broke it, and this is the result."

"But Baba," she cries bewildered, reverting to the name she called her mother when she was a tot unsteady on her feet in a world of giants, "Why kill so many? Why all of them? It doesn't make sense!"

Her mother turns away, kneeling in the shed to lift a bloodied mass from the ground. Over her shoulder she says sharply:

"Fetch a pail of water and a brush, girl."

Later that day, after Donitza has washed the last of the blood from the shed and those birds that were not ripped apart have been plucked, beheaded and gutted, she sits with her mother at the back of the house. Bees are moving between the herbs and a scent of lavender fills the air.

Her mother places her arm over her shoulder and the girl leans into her body, feeling her mother's protection.

"Each of the creatures has his unique spirit, my Sparrow," her mother says in a kinder voice. "The timid, peaceful mouse, the gregarious rat, the honest horse, the inquisitive kid. As for the fox, he is watchful and he is wily. Many say he is cunning. They are right about that. He can beguile and enchant with his pretty fur and delicate features. People love him for that, as if he is a hero. But they forget he has his own purpose. He is utterly self-serving."

A fat glistening bee emerges from the pink-white trumpet of a bellbine that winds its way up a bush nearby.

"But why kill so many?"

"Ha," she laughs, a tone of bitterness in her voice. "Because he is not so wily that he can rise above himself," she turns to face her daughter's puzzlement. "Some say that in the wild a fox capturing more than one bird would be a matter of great luck, so he would instinctively kill both. They say this is why, when he steals into the coop, he can't help but kill everything. Mother Nature would never be so bounteous, and so he follows his own nature and kills and kills and kills."

"This is what you mean, then? That he cannot rise above himself?"

"No, my Sparrow," her mother laughs. "I said that is what some people say. But those same people say that the fox is cunning, that he is clever and he is wise. How clever, then, how wise, is the fox who kills all his food in one day, when he could come back month after month and take one bird here and another there, so that you and I might not even notice?"

"What, then?" her daughter asks. "What do you mean he cannot rise above himself?"

Her mother draws herself up, tightening her arm protectively around the body of her daughter, takes a breath. She kisses the top of her daughter's head and says with sudden seriousness

"Despite all his art and cleverness, the fox has a weakness."

"What weakness?"

"For power."

"Why?"

"Because he cannot resist it. Even when he is in control, when he is the master of his kingdom in the shed, the hens his subjects – he cannot resist exercising his power."

Her mother withdraws her arm and with her hand gently turns the girl's head toward her, looking deep into her eyes.

"The time you are most in control is the time to exercise least power. Beware the fox. Learn from him, but do not keep him too close – and never play his tune."

*

In the precinct, the day is growing old. Donitza shivers in the half-light. A figure moves toward her, but she cannot see whom because her vision is blurred by tears. It comes closer, standing in front of her, not seeming to have a sense of personal space. Through the saltwater prism she has a momentary impression of a pair of thick glasses and soft eyes, and something hot breathing on her. Quickly she wipes her eyes, staring defensively, drawing a sharp intake of breath at the intruder's closeness.

A polystyrene cup is pushed into her hand, spreading warmth through her fingers.

"Cold," the man says.

It is the same young man who was watching her nervously

before. He is wearing thick glasses beneath a woollen hat, and has an awkward manner. *A syndrome of some sort, a name for saying in a learned way he's not quite right, makes him slow-witted maybe,* she thinks.

She takes him in warily. Men. Strangers who are men. They're the ones you have to watch out for, because the women, well, they're not usually violent. *Not usually.*

"Thanks," she says by reflex, but regrets it straight away. The way those intense eyes look at her, and how his face lights up. He stares at her for a few seconds longer than she is comfortable. They stand in the cold air, their coffee steam blending, their breathghosts twining. She steps away from him and he steps in again.

She feels angry. *Men.* Men who want to possess her like that ugly fool in the *Tavern,* thinking he's a pirate with his swagger and his big hat. She knew he would try to follow her out through the snow and from instinct stepped off the kerb into the ice-hard tyre tracks so he would not see where she had gone. *An ingrained instinct.* She's met bullyboys like him before. *Men.* She hates them.

"What do you want?" she challenges him loudly. "What are you doing?"

"Say thanks," he says. She smoulders at him.

"What? I just did, are you deaf..?"

But he cuts her off, struggling with his own awkwardness, his face screwed up. "I want to *say thanks.*"

She stops half way through her sentence. "What?"

He gazes at her, struggling with what he is feeling, fumbling for words. He points to her violin and blurts.

"Something in this. Makes me feel *funny.* My heart, it... it – it goes... faster."

He stands there continuing to look confused for two more heartbeats, then shrugs and looks away. In that second she senses something good in him. No threat from him. No desire for possession. No destruction. Just the meeting of a mind like the air or the rain coming to her. The rag and tag and hello and push and pull of life in the abstract. Not cruel. Just how it is. Beyond representation. The feeling surprises her.

He shrugs again, uncomfortable, as if his proximity to her pains him. "Maybe I'll hear you again."

Then he turns on his heel and walks away, his head down a little and his eyebrows raised above his glasses, as if he is somehow continually surprised by what the world has in store for him on the other side of them.

*

Watching the exchange between the young man and Donitza from the far side of the precinct is Riley. He sees her stance soften toward him as she watches him go – a slight dropping of the shoulders and relaxation of the body. He notes the way she inclines her head at an angle, and interprets that posture for what it is: curiosity.

He stands, studying her profile in the lowering light, the lampcast oranging the whited scene to alien contours around her, shadow gathering in snow pocks. He can't help but watch her.

For a moment he is overwhelmed by a sense of something extraordinary, a sense of something *other* that fills him with yearning. A sickly feeling that takes him back to childhood. Kids on the street playing together. An older girl with long hair. Obsessions drove him even then. *She is playing with her schoolfriends. She turns to him and smiles. He is grateful for that. Anything. He'll do anything. Another girl says something to her, nudges her, she laughs. He sinks in on himself, angry, powerless, hot with longing.* These feelings, the obsession, they have been reawakened by this foreigner in the snow. He is pulled along by her, his tide to her moon.

Riley looks from her to the object of her interest. This other man behind his glasses. What of *him?*

Riley considers him in his red hat as he walks away from her. Why would she talk with *that?* Why waste a second of her life on *that?*

Now Donitza glances over her shoulder across the precinct in his direction. *Always, she checks over her shoulder.* He has noticed this and is ready. He shrinks back, flat against glass, not wanting to be seen studying her. *What the fuck? Like a fucking moonstruck kid?!* She does not notice him, and he stays secreted despite himself, watching, obsessing. He runs a film in his head of how he will take her, but needs a plan of action to make it happen. This faltering, this is not him – he takes what he wants. But not from her. Somehow, not from her.

She has made it clear already she will not star in his movie willingly. The last few days when he has tried to speak with her in the pubs, she has repeated her reaction of that first night. Withdrawn, sullen, silent. When she avoids meeting his eyes, the act serves only to make him seek hers more. This is how he is. He sees, he wants. Always the same. He laughs at an idea: this woman in white looking like a bride. Mock vows come to him. *To have and to hold, with tightening grip. To possess and to use. Till Death, us –*

What *is* it about her? Something stops him getting what he wants. She is implacable but in a way he has never known. Inaccessible.

Foreign, he thinks, both repelled and fascinated.

He needs to know more.

When she gathers up her case and moves to leave, he follows.

*

Donitza walks, her shawled shoulders hunched against the cold, up to the north reach of the shopping precinct, past the hippy shop on the corner, and the hairdresser; flitting past warm-lamped shopfronts in the darkling day. Flakes again. A whirl and flurry. He is behind her, knowing the rhythm of when she will look back and stepping into shop fronts as he senses her about to turn. Thus they go, tracker and tracked, past the pub and the neat, bright coffee shops with after-work salespeople gathered for chats before their trudge home in the city's silence.

The snow falls faster.

East now, toward lines of houses in neat terraces along roads that in the summer are drenched in lazy sunshine and dust, or in the rain summon the redolent nose of tarmac.

The mothlike flakes create lampcast shadows, a mirror of whiteness and darkness above and below.

I'm losing her in the snow, he thinks, the whirl growing faster. *Weird. Like the snow's making it happen. - What the fuck!?*

A shape appears in his path, dark and half-seen, obscured by the blizzard. *Unreal, the way it's so blinding*, the feathers blowing frigid in upon him. He hears a high-pitched shout, like a cough – an animal barking – and sees ahead of him a fox, head down, blocking his way. Large, with white flakes settling along its back ridge, teeth bared. It barks again, its eyes green as the sea.

He stops in his tracks and shouts – "Piss off! Go on!"

The creature holds its ground, and Riley breathes deep a moment, the air stinging his nose. It barks once more and he steps forward to kick at it. His foot swings through empty air. The fox is a shadow thrown on the snow. *From where?* he looks around with startled eyes.

Ahead, the path is empty. No darkhaired violinist. Something on the back of his neck. A finger that lifts the hairs; a cold wind down the nape. For a breath's length he is afraid.

"Something weird about her," he says to the air. "Fuck!"

He turns, unsure of what he saw and heads to a pub to escape the cold and think on the apparition; an otherworldly moment on a pavement in a snowbound city.

*

Stepping in from the cold, Donitza pulls off her boots in the hallway, near the shelf and mirror where, most days, Celia checks if she looks presentable to the world before heading into it. Pulling off her fur hat, she shakes down her hair, running her white fingers through it, then freezes mid-movement, her eyes shooting up to noises from above. Light is seeping on to the landing, painting a line of brightness on the wall at the top of the stairs; she hears another movement and grows tautly alert. *Someone in my room.* She knows those rummaging noises from other, less homely places. *Going through my stuff. – Who? Even here?*

Instinctively, she pulls her boots back on, then pads up the stairs, clutching her violin case before her. Light is pouring from her room. She stiffens at a muttering sound, a low conversation. She goes to the door; its weight gives way under gentle pressure; she peers in.

Celia is reaching into the chest of drawers by the window. She lifts a jumper, looks at it a moment, then buries her lined face in the cloth. Hot tears; murmurings; gentle hushed mutterings. *A ritual? A prayer? Like my mother did, sometimes?* Celia pulls out a pair of black jeans, a swirl of stars on the fabric glitters in the yellow electric light. Celia says: "Yes, yes, here they are. Yes! My little love. My girl. Janey. You are still here, now. With me always."

"What are you doing in my room?" Donitza interrupts with half-accusation. Celia stands, looks around, her short hair in greys and whites – *like a fledgling gull.* She smiles, half apology, half something else. *What? Affection?* She looks younger than she did when Donitza first saw her – sliding on the packed snow in the precinct. As if she is breaking out from years of ice. There is joy in her, though her eyes are wet with tears.

"Ah. You're back," she smiles gently. "I was thinking about you. I thought you must need more clothes."

"I have clothes," Donitza answers.

"But not many," she points at the camouflage rucksack in the corner of the room. With an airy sweep of her hand she gestures the clothing she is half way through offering to the jutting mouths of drawers. "These clothes, these are Janey's. I think... she is very much like you. Her shape. You are so slender, like her. Would you like them? They are very warm..."

Donitza is uncomfortable with the emotions the clothes are washed in. She steps closer – garments neatly folded – socks and trousers, a pretty A-line skirt – a scarf in russet browns, gloves to match. They have a style to them, she notices – with a preference for creams and browns. *What does it mean that Celia has put them there?*

Donitza takes a breath in, holds it for two seconds, and pushes the breath out. She must take charge of her suspicious nature, after all. This stillness is a moment to recognise kindness. The act affects her more than she expects. Her throat tightens.

"I can't," Donitza says, straining against an emotional matrix. "They, they are special to you, I think."

Celia smiles and looks sad at the same time. "Yes, they are. That's why I'd like you to wear them, Janey –" She corrects herself. "Donitza. They are my granddaughter's. You're out in the cold, and you can't keep wearing the same old clothes day in, day out. They need to go in the wash. You need something to wear."

"I have others," she answers, patting her rucksack.

"But not many," Celia replies. "All worn out and in need of repair..."

Donitza's eyes widen at the intrusion. Who is this woman to have gone through her personal belongings? Before she can muster indignation in this foreign language, Celia walks to the square wardrobe in the corner of the room.

"There are these, too," she says, throwing it open and revealing a glittering array of dresses – greens, reds, bright colours in sumptuous cloths – striking summer dresses with halter necks, a peasant-style dress with a lace-up front in green. Donitza gasps. What a sense of presence this Janey has – what a sense of visuals.

Before she realises what she is doing, she puts her hand among them, feeling the softness of the fabrics, the way they caress her hand, smells the scent of material fresh despite years in store. Greedily, she draws out a long cableknit cream dress on its hanger, holds it against her – *a bodysleeve in wool!* – and looks down the line of her body. She has never seen anything like it, and she smiles to herself, the sensation causing her soul to lift, like air on a sun-warmed road.

A thought visits her.

"Celia, where is Janey, now?" she asks, fearing the answer. Celia falls quiet a while, her smile dropping as she withdraws into herself.

"Where is she now?" the old lady repeats. "Where? She went out one night. That's all I know. What more to say except – *I never saw her again.*"

"What? What do you mean?" Donitza asks.

The memories well up now inside the old woman – but though she wants to spill them out, she can't. The images and feelings are too intense. The night her teenaged granddaughter stepped into the summer's night. So hot, so close. *I'm heading out*, she said, *to get some cool air on my body.* One of those hot airless nights, when a high pressure had settled on the island, a great heavy bird warming its brood.

An image as clear as the night she lived it. Celia can see herself in her imagination, down by the sea in the moonlight. The police liaison officer telling her: *They found her clothes by the water.* But after that, nothing. Where she was, the police had no idea.

She remembers the yearning in her body, a kind of pull, as if her heart and all the soft tissue were being drawn out of her; the waking in the night, hoping her girl would come back to her, determined she would see her again. The tv appeals, the interest of the journalists, all dying away after a while. Till there was nothing. Nothing but this house, this feeling of emptiness. Hanging on through the years, still hoping that one day she will walk in through the door.

The flood of memories steals her voice.

Donitza can see the anguish. She sees how, in an attempt to dispel it, the older woman turns her head, rolling her neck in a circle to clear the images and sounds from her mind. She steps forward and holds the old woman close. A reflex response to which the other responds desperately, holding the younger, taller woman with pained tightness, her age-creased cheek pressed against

Donitza's. After a few minutes, Celia drops her arms and steps back, wipes her eyes, smiles at Donitza and reaches for one of the items in the wardrobe.

"Look at this. What do you think?"

The younger woman looks in admiration at the dark blue fabric of a long coat.

"It's lovely," she says and pulls it on.

Celia sighs and smiles again, her outbreath an exorcism.

"That's your colour, my dear. In fact, I'd say it's made for you."

An unspoken understanding goes between them.

"Thank you. Thank you!" says Donitza, her eyes shining in the electric light.

*

Another giver has been out dispensing more of his magic. Despite the snow, *business must go on*, he reflects, performing an audit of his clients.

Rich kids who are going to snort the Charlie he delivered, off the thighs of an accommodating escort at a pre-stag before they jet off to Prague tomorrow morning. Till recently, they attended the big private school jammed into the top of the old town. He appreciates the way these boys expect others to do what they tell them, and for their needs to come absolutely first. He *gets* them. He is one of them. Then there are the kids on the estates in the middle of town, wanting pills and a buzz out of a life already tired with itself. There is the accountant in the big house overlooking the sea who likes to throw a party and make every pleasure possible available to his young friends. In the restaurant quarter, the Chinese prostitutes and their pimps working from well-appointed buildings with cameras over the door. How he got that gig, he doesn't know. In-fighting between rival Chinese groups and somehow he got to supply. There it is: *coals to Newcastle*. Then, there's the teacher in one of the more suburban streets who needs to de-stress as he enters a new term of *crowd control*. The builder who likes to get away from the wife and kids on a Saturday night; the judge seeking something special to please his favourites – a taste for boyflesh he picked up at a smart school all those years before, which now leads him, literally, to chase not-too-elusive youth through the house in games of love. The exhausted chef at one of the smart restaurants down at the harbour who needs something just to stay awake. The police inspector who needs it to maintain the rhythm of his life – he fell into it instead of counselling (because that would go on his file) after his wife left him. Each wants something a little different: some fixed on one substance, others trying whatever comes to hand.

His is a democratic appeal. Beside the high-achievers and middle-incomers and the lost young are the lowest of the low, who spend the very last penny of their benefit on his medication. These he views with contempt – confused souls who don't quite know how they came to be where they are, but seek to step out of a life of uncertainty and abuse into a few brief hours of forgetfulness, when the boundaries of self are dissolved or obliterated. They cut and cut his powder, and sell to each other to raise the money to buy from him.

One of them today even said something that made him want to puke. Seeing his own situation, the boy had raised his eyes as if seeking absolution and said: "Look, I'm not a bad person. Not really. Just – you know – like most of us. Trying to get by. Just getting by. That's why I do this." Then he had taken the packet, to cut it with washing powder and offer to his peers neurological problems in later life. *Not a bad person. Nah. Course not.* As if Riley gave a shit.

He considers his influence on their consumerist lives. Some are undoubtedly hooked, some employ his services from time to time, some are convinced they aren't addicted at all, though they are in far deeper than they imagine.

Business. It is so simple: find a need; supply it. Just like any other business. He doesn't *need* to be selling white powder or pills – something, anything to make their lives pass by more easily. Yet this commodity has the greatest influence. That is the key to repeat custom. He could be selling food or clothes – but though there are shoe addicts, they are less easily made. His is a brutal, biological economics. *Science.* He likes this thought. It is backed up with the cold rationale of numbers.

And yet, what he feels isn't cold. What Riley feels the passion for, the thing that drives him on, is the way his customers become reliant on him. They need him, and can't help themselves. They are, in the end, beneath him. That is where the warmth lies.

So he goes on, delivering his little packets of white-powdered enslavement to an ever-grateful world.

*

That night, Donitza is picking her way deftly over the ice on her way to another session. She is wearing the wool dress that hugs her body with a network of warmth, a slip beneath it, long boots with thick stockings, and over the top, hanging open because it looks somehow filmic that way, the long dark blue coat. She feels strange in these clothes, as if she is at once not quite herself, and more so. She is growing, she feels, growing and changing. The fit is surprisingly good; she finds that the dress hugs her body in a way that makes her more aware of it.

Ahead, paddling awkwardly over the ice, she sees the strange, awkward young man again, in his funny red woollen hat. The elastication has gathered a tight knot on the crown. He leans forward, peering through his glasses at the world ahead, that comical look of surprise on his face. His hands are red raw even in the lamplight, from one of the places where he works; a small hotel where he washes worktops in the kitchen, makes beds in the day, sweeps, cleans, scrubs, mends – keeping him just solvent, working compulsive cleanliness through the hotel.

From a corner, another figure appears. Tall, swaggering, dressed in black, engrossed in a message on his mobile. He and the smaller man collide. From a distance she sees the tall man round on the shorter one, cutting the air with aggressive movements, while the smaller man throws out his arms in forlorn appeasement. At his instant submission, the taller man laughs, then snatches his red woolly hat by the knot. The other grasps in the air, a child baited in the playground.

Protective rage rises inside her. She strengthens her stride, and as she approaches the two men, shouts, "Leave him! Leave him alone!"

The taller one jerks, straightens and turns to the shape striding toward him, drops the hat and steps back. She emerges into the light, moving from silhouette to 3D. He turns and stumbles across the road, hurrying in the direction of the pub. She looks after him, hands on hips, contemptuous – and puzzled.

Stooping, she picks up the young man's hat and hands it to him. He says nothing, takes it, blinking, shaking a little.

"Are you okay?" she asks him.

He turns on her – "Yes! Yes! Leave me alone!" – then scurries off in the snow.

His head is down again and he is bent low, intent on speed. She watches him go, this funny awkward man in his early 20s, skinny, with bad co-ordination. She feels something she has not felt before. She is not attracted to him. He is not attractive at all. But she recognises that he is kind and he is upset. The magic of his kindness makes a sympathetic patch of kindness in her. She can see that now. It surprises her and intrigues her – *fellow feeling*.

She strides after him. "Wait, don't go," she says. "Just stay a moment..."

He paddles on in the night, slipping on the ice in his awkward way. Then, realising she is steadier on her feet than him, he relents and looks back as she approaches, her violin case slung over her shoulder. The panic gone, he recognises her, and his shoulders sink again in submission.

"Are you going to play?" He asks, nodding to the case.

"Maybe," she says. "In the *King Street*." She tips her head sideways and backwards over her shoulder. "Coming?"

He wavers, wondering whether to follow. "I can't go in there," he gazes at the direction in which Riley disappeared, though he is half-tempted by the promise of hearing her play again. He dithers, basking in her moonglow, her white radiance, and feels a wordless fluttering in his heart. But this is not regular, not right. An intrusion in his life. He makes a decision. "I have to go. Somewhere to go," he turns again.

"Where?" she asks. "Where do you have to go?"

"I have to go," he repeats more firmly, and walks away from her, south, toward the sea, picking his way over the ice with his uncoordinated gait. She watches him for a while, then turns and walks the other way, picking back over the exchange.

Nothing unwanted in his look. No flirtation. Just interest in her. And a kind of... what? *Delight at seeing me, even in the panic?* It surprises her that this man should be so innocent.

I was a child, she thinks, *the last time I experienced something as simple as a hello that came without judgement or agenda. A child.*

She thinks of the cram of people that will be waiting for her in the pub, and how they are transforming into friends, these musicians. Or fellow travellers, in the way that musicians are, who join you on your journey from the opening notes of a melody to the end, and then disembark and go elsewhere. *My mother told me to play*, she says to herself. *Whenever I can. It was a promise I made her.*

She pictures herself – the little *Sparrow* playing in a long skirt – an ethnic outfit with a black swirl pattern on a faun background. A stream with sunlight upon it, the sparkle reflecting in her eyes. This image has not surfaced since she first lived it and she rocks back for a moment at its intensity.

She looks back again to where the man is walking, but he is a distant figure moving between sodium and shadow, and then he is gone.

*

Donitza considers. His inwardness, his lack of desire, intrigues her. She decides to follow him, setting aside her mother's injunction, and feeling a sense of transgression as she steps forward. With her violin case slung over her back on a strap, she is a huntress, tracking her prey through the snowbound streets.

She has a knowledge of snow. She understands it and can read it. His footsteps are easily recognisable in the white powder. Loping and uneven, with short strides, the toes digging in more heavily than the heels. She follows them like this down a narrow Georgian street; they punctuate the left hand side of a wider road before they skirt the Common. A long straight road. She can see him in the distance ahead, the sodium lamps reflecting from his coat, making of it a dull nothing colour. His red hat, bobbing as he makes his way, is flattened to grey–brown.

She walks more quickly, tracking him along the edge of the sea, coming eventually to the eastern pier, down-at-heel and deserted, piles of white collected over the arches on the windows, looking as if it has been decorated with cotton wool. It is a cloud of pleasure, a ruin of amusements, a palace abandoned to the winter ravages.

Still he goes on and she follows, the sound of the sea in their ears hard as steel on the metal shingle. As she passes the frozen lake, he is fifty metres ahead of her, crossing the glassy road. Skidding and slipping, he traverses a car park and comes to a metal doorway in the side of a hill.

He reaches in his pocket, unlocks the door, lets himself in and closes out the night.

She comes to the door and stops, studying it, hands on hips again, elbows jutting. An earthworks buried beneath snow looms above her. She walks around it to survey it, crunching through the deep layer of whiteness up to her knees, feeling the cold air on her face, the ice overtopping her boots in a chill ring. She walks past snowmen on the Common, and a line of beach huts in a straight row, opposite the sea, where the water shatters on the stones. She enters a space enclosed by walls, a separate haven of silence intersected by pathways lined by the snow-softened geometry of buried flowerbeds. Out the other side, she is by the earthworks again, completing the circuit. A mound of some sort, with no way in other than that metal door. She peers through the gap between door and jamb, and sees the inside open to the sky. *Not a mound at all, a walled space.*

She will climb, she decides, scuffing up a ramp of piled soil and snow.

As she ascends, she remembers when she was a little girl, coming back to her mother's house down the mountainside – the birds falling silent in the trees as she approached, *something in the scene watchful, expectant.* Later that day her mother asked her the question again.

"No mother, I didn't hear anything," she says. "There is nothing."

"Nothing," comes the reply. "That is the problem."

The exchange appears in a flash as she climbs and kneels atop the earthworks. *More of my past,* she thinks with something akin to panic, but is soon directed from her thoughts when she finds herself surveying a tiny village below.

Floodlights are on, illuminating minute houses, a church, a pub, a frozen stream in which a boat sits icelocked beside a row of neat country cottages. All this beneath a line of massive denuded trees, dwarfing the village below, silhouettes against a starry sky.

The young man is moving among the houses, clearing snow from the drives and pathways, checking that everything is clean and tidy, squinting while giving particular attention to one building, which he leans over and eyes closely. With a soft brush, he wipes snow from its roof, a benign giant in a fairytale. She can see his face in the light, attentive and calm, animated with a dedicated certainty she would not have believed of him.

He lifts a tiny car from the road, examines it, tuts and bobs off to a small room at one end of the compound. The entire village, surrounded by snowbound walls is a dwarf's grotto. A sacred precinct.

He disappears inside. A fluorescent light flickers, and she moves along the top of the wall to steal a better view. She can see him, bent over a table working at something. She leans to peer closer.

It is then her foot slips. She slides in the snow, careering and scrabbling down the bank, and landing in a heap on the floor with a shout and a winded groan.

He emerges from the workshop and runs toward her, brandishing a hammer, shouting, "No, no, keep away. You can't come here!"

She braces at the danger, reaching in the snow for something to defend herself, while a frigid gust brings in a flurry of flakes that pelt him from the branches. She stares up with aggressive eyes as he stands frozen, looking down on her, a whirl of confusion in his head, trying to compute this new arrival and fit her into his world scheme.

"You're going to hit me?!" she asks. "I only wanted to see where you go."

He lowers the hammer to his side, his surprised eyes staring a while longer before he exhales:

"It's cold. Come and have a cup of tea." Then, turning to her with a serious look, he says: "Watch where you put your feet. You nearly killed the Post Office."

She picks up her violin case, dusts off the snow, slings it over her back and follows him through the model village to the work room where the light glows. In the narrow precincts of this complex that was once a fortress, Donitza notices how his movements are less uncertain, more purposeful. Her breathghost dances in the brightness, spreading palely through night air as she steps into the warmth, unaware of how cold she is until the room's comfort embraces her.

On a tall stool by a workbench she perches to look at tiny figures of people, the broken shapes of two miniature houses in mock-Tudor styling, and more crushed people looking forlornly at what life has dealt them through no fault of their own. She wonders what he does in here, considering him silently as he stands by her, his back to her, a hammer in his hand.

She remembers a snippet - her mother talking of the dolls some use to bring illness on others, and the power of sympathetic magic. *A doll of wax. Push a pin into its eyes, the cursee is made sightless.*

She can hear the certainty and belief in her mother's voice again: "This is the practice of some who use sympathetic magic for their own ends. A single hair from the cursee's head is all you need. A hot knife to the poppet's eyes also induces blindness. The principles are the same as for the healing methods I have shown you. Never do this, my Sparrow. Magic used in this way always has consequences. Always."

While he fishes a dripping teabag from a cup, she picks up a tiny figure to examine – a police officer in old-fashioned dark blue tunic and high helmet. Donitza wonders: *Is this what he does here? Bad magic?*

He turns to her, asking: "Do you want milk – *put that down!*"

He steps over to her and takes it from her with a gentle movement.

"The glue isn't dry yet."

"Oh, sorry," she says, scrutinising him with wide, perceptive eyes. *He mends people*, she thinks, and says quietly:

"Milk, yes. No sugar."

"Here."

He hands her a steaming cup and sits at the workbench, all intensity as he lifts a tiny pin and gently taps together a corner of a mock-Tudor house. He loses himself in the work, gathering together minute splintered pieces and gluing them into a whole.

He doesn't say anything for 4 minutes. There is a large round clock on the wall above him, and with a childlike pleasure Donitza watches its hands progress. There is a kind of comfort here. Like an escape, and she resonates with it. The world outside his task has disappeared. To him she has disappeared, too, she realises, so she speaks again just to remind herself she is here.

"What are you doing?"

He starts at her voice, his look of surprise more surprised than before.

"Fixing things," he mutters under his breath, perhaps even annoyed.

"What is this place?" she persists.

He sits up, looking straight ahead, his eyes wide and alert.

"It's the village," he says. "The Model Village." He looks excitement and pride at her, all in one wave of emotion. "You never been here?"

"Never," she says, shrugging her shoulders.

"Let me show you," he says. "A tour."

He takes her hand and pulls her excitedly back out into the night, animated with a child's delight. He shows her the place where she landed, the Post Office, the neat line of houses, the butcher, the baker, the candlestick maker. There is a big house, where the lord of the manor lives and there is a harbour, now frozen solid, with a model boat. In the summer, it bobs around a narrow stream, plying its way forever through a landscape of giant grasses and miniature plastic trees, watched by the towering figures of children, their heads silhouetted against the sun.

It is a world here, a tiny community, with a castle, houses, shops, a school and a playing field. Neatly manicured lawns, a pub and all the things an English village needs.

"This is home," he says, his eyes glowing as he shows her round, her cup of tea pluming steam into the air as they go, as if she is a tourist arriving in a locomotive from the 1950s.

He looks up at the high walls – an old fort that has stood on that spot for hundreds of years, at first among the furze bushes and marshes of the Great Morass, and in later times, on the Common, always close to the eternal restlessness of the sea. A stable, solid world peopled by the garrison ghosts who once lived here. "It needs me," he tells her, proudly.

His face now passionate and sure is no longer lost in the unmanageable world of full-size streets outside, and she realises that for him it is all about scale. It is the carrying of his own thin limbs in a massive world that is his greatest fear. He gangles as if even his body is too large for him, and so he wants his world to mirror the sense of smallness inside himself.

"What do you mean, it needs you?"

His face falls of a sudden, and he looks sad anger at her. "I'm the guard," he says. "The local kids, when they get drunk, they climb over the walls and smash it. It's my job to make sure it isn't smashed. I look after it."

She is surprised. "You own this place?"

"Own it?" he looks back at her as if he has no idea what she means.

"Well, are you paid for this?"

He shrugs, uncomfortable at the question.

"In the summer, when the place is open. Kids came in one night and wrecked it. So I slept here and kept it safe. The owners didn't know. I was the cleaner who arrived early in the morning. I look after it all the time, like that." With a conspiratorial inflexion he explains: "I kept a key." He shoots an imploring look. "You won't tell, will you?"

So it is that throughout the winter the village's plastic inhabitants have seen him come in to clear the snow, preventing the roofs collapsing under its weight. They have seen him bring order to their world. He brings care. It provides a focus for his natural kindness.

He fires at her a flurry of unexpected facts. Minuscule details about where the models came from, how old they are, the constant struggle for security and how, when visitors come, you never can tell who will arrive next. Mothers, children, old people, tourists, dads, couples, people breaking up, people in love. An unending stream of people. All the world is here.

While he talks, Donitza pales; she is looking at a slope, covered with snow, tiny models of pine trees upon it.

She is there again. Pulled back down the long tunnel of remembrance to the little house where she lived as a child.

Her mother looks from the window, turns to her and asks: "Did you hear anything?"

Shrugging her shoulders, Donitza says, "No mama. No. There is nothing."

Her mother can sense something. She doesn't know what it is, but she stays frozen, looking out of the window for four whole minutes. Donitza counts the minutes on the clock on the wall. Then her mother shakes her head and mutters something to herself.

Later, Donitza gets up and goes to the sink – a handpump over a stone trough in the corner of the kitchen that looks out over the back garden. In the summer there would stand neat rows of flowers and herbs, thyme, parsley, sage, tarragon, coriander. Further off, the other plants her mother cultivates: wormwood, mandrake, valerian, southernwood, sorrel and many more too. On their far side, the garden falls away, a steep drop to the valley floor. – *The plants are all buried in the snow*, she thinks to herself. – *It is a miracle the water hasn't frozen.*

She lifts a glass to pour herself water and then, noticing something through the window, turns to her mother.

"Mama, is there a fire in the valley?"

Her mother's head shoots up from her work at the table, her face drawn and pale. She stands, alert.

"A fire?" she repeats, a tremor in her voice.

Donitza pulls herself back to the present with a jolt and looks at the young man.

"I don't know your name," she says, desperate to extract herself from her memories.

"Edward," he replies. "But Eddy. If you see what I mean."

"Well I want to thank you, for the tour, Eddy," she says, aware of the uncomfortable closeness of the pictures pushing in on her everyday world. "Now I owe you two hot drinks." She turns, looking for a way out.

He imagines he has bored her, and has a pang of something, he is not sure what. *Loneliness?* The sudden fear of a final goodbye, a figure vanishing across what he perceives as vast fields of snow surrounding this silent space? Will she come back again? With an urgent move, he steps over to her, unexpectedly taking her hand. She is surprised by his repeated touch and not displeased.

"There's something I should show you," he says with puppydog eagerness. Those surprised eyes under the glasses drill into her. "It's special. Very special."

Reflexively, she shakes her hand loose and steps back from him, feeling the snow on the grass crunch under her feet, as the moon, huge and white, sails out from behind a cloud and fills this Eden with a white, ghostly light. Memories are flooding back in; a tide of forgotten things. She suppresses them again, giving herself over to his insistence in an effort to stop the sounds and sights pressing and clamouring inside her.

"Sure," she says. "Why not?"

He beckons her to follow, and they walk to an iron gate on one side of the compound. It is old and heavy with a massive lock. On the far side a black tunnel stretches away to nothingness.

"In here," he says, excitedly, his voice echoing in the tunnel's mouth, deepened by its shadows. "It's right in here." He unlocks the gate and pulls it open so it gives a juddering screech in the white night. He vanishes into the blackness. "Come!" he says, his words fractured by ice and stone, and she imagines for a moment that a child's night-monster waits in its lair.

The fancy quelled, she follows, her eyes stretched wide. She finds no light and nothing to hold her attention. One step forward. Another. It is even colder in here, and she feels her skin under the woollen dress pimple up, puckering and tightening on her body, pushing her hardening nipples against her clothes so her skin almost hurts. Her hair is standing up.

She can hear him panting ahead. Despite her misgivings, she steps onward, darkness whirling around her. His loud breathing echoes from the confining walls where, a hundred years or more before, the garrison stored its victuals. As her eyes adjust, a residual glimmer of moonlight reveals the tunnel has a low arched roof, the walls bending over her, inspecting her, disapproving of her, perhaps. She puts up her hands to defend against the coarse brick – cold, rough and hard beneath her palms.

Ahead, she hears a click, and the room jumps into fluorescent brightness – hard white and blue – making her wince with pain. She brings her hand over her eyes.

Then she gasps.

There, ahead of her, stands something in a glass case incongruous and spectacular. Eddy looks from it to her proudly, then back at it. The tunnel's end has a room spreading out to 4 metres square and three metres high. On a podium in a glass case, stands a model of the town's Guildhall, with its columns, its grand steps and frieze. A perfect, two metre tall replica, made entirely of –

"Matchsticks," he says excitedly, catching sight of the surprise on her face. "It is made of matchsticks. Can you believe it!?" He claps his hands, a simple boyish joy on his face.

His enthusiasm is infectious. Donitza laughs out loud at him and his delight. She feels safe here with this strange young man, a giant among the tiny places of the world.

"Did you make this?" she asks in wonder.

He laughs excitedly. "No. No... It was here when I got here. I look after it," he explains.

"Wait," she says, raising her finger as a sudden thought takes her, then unslings the violin case from her shoulder with well-practised fingers. "The acoustics here, they are perfect."

She plays a melody – a tune from the Balkans, that blows in as if from the mountains, and echoes around the tunnel, filling the night with its sad tale, with its suffering and overcoming, telling a story of infinite sorrow – and of light in the woods, the tiniest hope, that leads to a safe world of eternal beauty.

He blinks at her, as if he has never seen a creature on Earth like her.

That is because he hasn't.

*

Riley scans the faces in *The King Street*, wondering where *the Witch* has gone. That is what he calls her now. The nickname grew from that uncanny moment when she disappeared ahead of him while he was distracted by a shape he can't explain. It was reinforced in that odd shadow-confrontation when she emerged into lamplight from darkness. Something about her spooked him. Her, in that woollen dress – that *body sock*, as he calls it. Did he imagine something else? Moving behind her, a figure in the darkness. *A presence. Something that followed her as she walked toward him?* Or was it just her shadow, stretching away behind her, a massive figure of a woman, or an animal? It freaked him, like the other shadow he saw earlier.

"Bad *white powder?*" he asks himself in a moment of self knowledge. Something cut with the coke that's making him lose his perspective? PCP, maybe? He'll speak with his supplier. Or he'll beat the shit out of him. Then in a looping thought – *Is this paranoia?* – A question that makes him more paranoid until he shakes it off to focus on his obsession:

The Witch.

The name is only half a joke. He looks across at the tangle of musicians, nods to those who buy from him, and realises how offbalance she makes him. *Her otherness, her unattainability* – and simultaneously – how familiar she seems.

The music night is not unwinding as it usually unwinds, with Riley making his oppressive presence felt. He usually has a way of getting plugged in at an open mic night. It's not all bullying and bleeding ears. He is skilled on the guitar, in a brutal way, and can back others – he will, for example, support lone singers in need of a musician, though somehow he makes the accompaniment about himself and not about them. He provides guitar solos for other ensembles, though they go on too long, are unsubtle and loud. He can provide an energy that drives a night forward, especially when there is no-one else there to take the slack. This is why he manages to stay central to the music scene, though he is not liked. And he gets his way. Begrudgingly MCs submit to him, because he is half-justified in demanding to play. And they wouldn't say no. *Oh, no.*

Tonight, Riley can't get into the music, so, with a flourish, he walks out, carrying his guitar in his case, pensive, unsettled.

He shivers through the streets, his route taking him past a kebab van on one corner, down through the wealthier part of the city toward the lake. Soon, he is standing outside his mother's house again. *Back here.* As if an irresistible line has hooked him and tugs him always here, near *the sea, the black, black sea.*

Fresh snow begins to fall. Far off on the tide a ship moves through the dark water – the massy presence of a block of flats, a city in itself, carrying holidaymakers from the weather-announcer's *heavy snow flurries* toward the continent. They are heading south in search of warmth, the place where the sparrows go, migrated souls.

Go on, piss off. Just piss off and leave. The thought comes from nowhere.

Why is he angry? He looks inside himself to see only night. He wavers, considering clattering into the house and waking his mother, who will be sitting in a chair, head nodded as always, as if waiting for someone to return. Then, as he is about to walk away, he notices a movement near the lake. A figure walking through the snow.

The slim body; the steady-graceful movements.

It's her.

Before he knows he is doing it, he crouches to watch her go. His legs soak in the snow through his jeans.

Why crouch? He can't understand it, except that the sight of her earlier, emerging into three dimensions from silhouette shocked him.

He eyes her in that long blue coat, that hat. She is engrossed in something, and doesn't look around her like she normally does. He lets her pass, then stands, and wonders why she is crossing the park, now, this late, on her own. *Where has she been? Why wasn't she at the pub?*

He goes over to her solitary line of footprints, and stands looking in the direction the toe-arch is pointed and then back where the heel has come from. He considers following her, but wavers, nape hairs rising again, as they did when he saw the fox shadow barring his way. *Who is this woman?* He needs more information and traces her footsteps backwards, backwards through the snow toward the fort. The trail ends at its doorway, where her ghost in his mind's eye steps through, turns, closes it and goes.

There is a glimmer inside. He bangs on the door, a series of repeated slaps with the palm of his hand.

The young man he saw earlier opens the door, smiling, "You've come back – you forgot your gloves..."

With a violent shove Riley surges over him, sending him sprawling backwards, a pair of hands gripping him as he falls on the frozen ground. He drags him roughly along a concrete path, kicking and struggling, pulling him back into the fort.

Eddy is screaming, clawing at the ground, a flurry of white panic rising around him.

*

A handful of rogue flakes scatter from the sky as Donitza arrives back at the neat terraced house in the grid of Victorian houses.

She goes through to the back, takes something from the fridge and opens the door to a back garden that is perhaps five metres long and four metres wide. Figurines inhabit the snowbound bushes. A cherub eyes her from below knee height from a holly bush, a concrete cat sleeping in stone-cold ice keeps a lazy eye open, a fox unmoving by the shed. She buries her fingers in the packet of bacon and throws strips out onto the snow while she sings a light airy melody. The fox detaches from the shadow and edges toward her. It stiffens and sniffs the air, narrowing its eyes, then steps forward and bolts the bacon hungrily. She looks to its red fur and sends a wave of comfort out to it.

"Friend?" she asks in her own language, a word muffled by the snow.

It eyes her, as if understanding, holding her gaze for a moment in its green eyes before dipping its head and turning away.

Snow, always snow, she thinks, remembering how much she has seen in her life. But there wasn't always snow. In the thawing of memories that have begun on this island, she remembers summers of blistering heat when it felt like the trees would spontaneously burst into a dance of flame. But winter is stamped on her soul. Snow is a home to her; something in it reassures her, as if its cold embrace is who she is. When it falls, she feels safe. The snow around her silent and white, an anaesthetic blanket in which to numb herself.

She starts, as a gull, lost in the night, gives a cry among the flakes. The clouds are thinning now; holes appearing; stars peer through. *Are some birds made of snow?* She asks herself in the soft language of home. *Are their feathers snowflakes, spiralling out of the sky?*

Something about the snow today is not numbing. As if a new wind has blown in, a warmer wind at last that moves across the icescape of her interior. It touches her with warm hands. *Fellowship.*

The bent old woman Celia; the strange young man Eddy. Always she has drifted, but now she feels an extranatural sense that perhaps... is she..? Has she begun to put down the shallowest roots beneath the ice?

Eddy, she thinks the name with a smile as she closes the door after the fox slinks away.

"As if he is the village guardian and yet he is the fool!" she says to the kitchen before she makes her way upstairs.

Who do I think I am? She feels a terrible sadness as she remembers her promise to him that she will see him tomorrow. Surprised eyes delighted that she agreed to sit with him in the fort and talk and make coffee. *Is this what I am?* She asks herself, catching sight of herself in the long mirror in her bedroom. *So damaged I trust only a simpleton?*

Yet perhaps it is a simpleton she needs. A holy fool. No family, but someone to be at least familiar.

She undresses and switches off the light, the room drenched in moonlight.

*

It comes back to her.

When she was a child there were some nights when her mother would wake her to the full moon shining in the sky through the pine trees. Even in the summer, the air up here was often cool at night, though in the day it felt as though the sun focussed his light on her house through a lens. In the vast chasm of the night the stars were yellow, large and flickering. Her mother would point out the constellations that swayed the virtues of the plants that grew around her. She would recite recipes of spells, over and again.

"Mistress Aconita and the Red King must swim together to give birth to the Water of Life," she would tell her daughter. "This is how the virtues unite: in the cauldron," and as she said these things, she would cut the Wolfbane from selected patches where the moon lay in pools around the house.

The house sat on the edge of the valley side, looking warily from its perch at the dome of the mosque below, and at the square tower of the church in the middle distance on the far side of the river. Both were still dimly visible even in the moonlight. Nodding toward these buildings her mother had once told her how the people who went to them claimed that all were descended from one man whose name in the ancient language signified the word "red". This she said was the colour of the clay from which a potter had made the Red Man, whom they believed was the First Man.

They had strange beliefs. For example, they hated the one they called the Bringer of Light and called him the Enemy yet worshipped a child born near the time of the shortest day, who symbolised the reborn sun, and whom they addressed as The Light of the World. Strangely, too, the Enemy, this Bringer of Light, was often pictured in their beliefs as a Red Man. She shook her head and laughingly said: "They have forgotten so much that what they remember makes them angry and confused. It is best to have little to do with their ideas." Then, after a moment's thought her mother turned to her pointedly: "It is true that when the Red Man comes, calamity circles nearby, casting black shadows, like carrion crows."

Not far off, a stream tumbled down a scarp toward the valley floor, and her mother would gather water from it in jars at certain times of the night with incantations and songs and leave them to grow miraculous life from nothing. Donitza would marvel how the water would be clear when it was gathered, but within a few days the green scum of life would line it. Later fish would move within it, and tadpoles. Eventually frogs would chirrup and bloat from the jars, and when these came her mother, with a childish smile to her daughter, would kiss them before releasing them into the wild.

"You never know, do you? If one is a prince?" And she would throw back her head and laugh at such times, showing her pearl white teeth to the sky and her long, narrow, beautiful face would turn up to the light and receive the sun's kiss.

There never was a prince.

One day her mother pointed at the water in one of the jars and said, "Look, my Flower, look". A stone had formed in the water overnight. It was floating half suspended. She fished it out with her fingers and held it in her hand, her face illumined by wonder. It was tiny, perhaps only 3 centimetres long, light blue like a dawn sky and mottled black. Her mother put it on a bed of straw on a shelf over the stove to keep it warm.

After three days and nights, the stone began to rock, at first with slight movements, but over time with increasing strength. As Donitza watched, her mouth wide open, a beak broke through. It was not a stone, but an egg that hatched to reveal a bird. Not a wet, straggling chick as she had seen from the hens in the garden, but a perfectly-formed bird with oil-blue-green feathers. It gave three chirrups and flew away.

As it did so, her mother took on a serious air: "Life is in a constant process of transformation," she said with a low, melodious tone. "Ice, water, stone. One thing becomes something else becomes something else becomes something else. It is best to talk about life not as *being*, but as *becoming*."

Later she continued this serious mood, and said: "When the snows come in the winter, ice can sometimes stop the cycle, but only for a short time. Ice brings death to the land. Yet death, too, is a part of the cycle of becoming. That is a lesson we all must learn."

Her daughter listened with a cocked head, and wondered at the bounty her mother had given her. She considered again the virtues of Aconite, and how Bird's Foot is governed by Saturn, being good for the healing of wounds. She could describe over 500 plants and their virtues and the planets that govern them, and to whom they are wed and where they make their houses – in high places and low, in wet and dry, on land in water or in the branches. She could recount numberless decoctions and infusions, and the plants that could bind, blind and enhance. Purgatives and the soporifics; healers of wounds and givers of visions. There were spells too which gave special protection.

"The werewolf is feared by most in these parts," her mother once told her as she sat bathed in firelight in a clearing outside their nightbound hut, her face angled to the full moon. "His pack will surround a house if he detects a human presence, and break in and devour all inside. He will find his way into the cellar and drink it dry, piling barrels to the ceiling to show that these are no common wolves." Then with her eye upon her daughter she added: "Tonight is a night for werewolves, in which the Goddess releases the beast in the man. But the werewolf will not bother you because you are under the protection of Euterpe, whose music makes the savage beast sleep. This is the power in your music."

She held up the fiddle in the night, as if offering it to the moon. "There is protection here. Integral to the cycle of becoming is the hub at the centre. As the hub turns, it transmits the music of the spheres, which unite all under the rule of harmony." She looked severe. "But without harmony, the world loses shape and the rim falls to the centre."

As her mother said this she held her long dark hair against her neck, while the firelight bathed her in its golden light, turning her eyes to yellow slits.

"In the cycle of becoming, the werewolf is just one of the more extreme examples," her mother went on. "Transformation must not be stopped. A melody never quite repeats itself in the same way. A dirge may turn to a song of marriage and become a dance. Nothing stays the same. The adept of Euterpe, she is safe in the centre. Create the magic circle. An enclosed space that means safety. Protection, too, is part of the cycle."

As if to prove her point, she sang a long slow melody into the darkness; and, to Donitza's amazement, she saw the eyes of the night creatures reflect back from the eaves. There was a rustling and movement in the forest, then a quietness. The creatures blinked, an audience waiting. Then came a sound in the distance of something massy and savage crashing through the woods. Donitza tensed, as her mother sang again, a high pitched note, dropping low till it pulsed in her chest.

A wolf sprang from the forest edge, fixing them with fierce yellow eyes. Donitza jumped to her feet, opening her mouth to shout, but with a subtle move of her hand her mother cautioned her to silence and bade her sit.

With a curious gaze the wolf came to her, sniffing around the fire, before standing before her mother. She held out her hand and the creature licked it gently.

"Poor soul," her mother said quietly. "Poor soul to have the moon madness upon you. We are your friends."

This woman, this was her mother.

*

A bright morning spreads over the whiteness of the town. The sun, putting its hot hands on the edge of the world, pulls itself up over the island, peering like a child over the flat surface of a table. The ice-locked world relaxes imperceptibly as those gentle fingers of light reach their way into the morning. Victorian lamps blink off as the daylight comes, their glass panels caked with ice. In one quarter, gulls shiver and huddle, scavenging among black bin bags, and gathering by the fume extraction pipes of the restaurants above them. On the north of the island, a small pond is a solid lump of ice, and children have taken to skating across it, joyous in the face of worried men in yellow jerkins who try to stop them.

The elderly look from their windows, wondering when this will end. Some of them think back to other big freezes, like '47 and '63 when air frosts left icicles hanging from sagging telephone cables and waterpipes cracked across the city. They wonder if the sunlight is the start of the end of it all.

Donitza rises with a brightness in her eye and sits with Celia at breakfast, smiling to herself.

Celia, long experienced in the ways of women, notices the vibration coming from the younger woman with interest.

"What will you do today?" she asks, in her ritual way.

Donitza looks up from her coffee, which she has been absently stirring, a smile on her face. She shrugs.

"I don't know," she answers evasively. "See the town. Maybe. Meet some people."

Celia sits back, a piece of toast in her hand; she takes in the young woman with knowing eyes.

A fellah, she thinks. *How lo-o-vely!*

She twinkles at the younger woman across the table but knows not to say anything – this young woman is so defensive. But then, unable to stop herself, she blurts out:

"Well you two have a lovely time," to which Donitza jerks back her head enough to confirm Celia's surmise, and they exchange a smile of understanding.

*

Donitza feels light. It is a feeling she has not experienced for a long time. As she makes her way through the streets toward the sparkling sea, she feels as if her feet are not quite touching the snow. It makes little sense to her, this sudden breaking of mood, just from a shared tea and a toy village in the snows, but she feels good.

A flash of more recent remembrance. As she made her way home across the snow the previous night, wrapped in her long blue coat, she looked up to see the white moon appear in a frozen sky patched with stars between the clouds. The stars were not hot nor yellow, as they were when she was a child in the mountains, but distant and small and she wondered then if actually the entire night were dotted with pure, perfect, clean shards of ice.

Today, as she comes across the glittering field to the low fort where she sat and talked and played the night before, she thinks of transformation, as her mother once told her.

Arriving at the iron doors to the Model Village, she knocks upon them, and is disappointed that the simpleton does not answer. He said he would be there, but he is not.

She walks around the fort, tempted to climb over to the citadel inside, but she can sense his absence. Disquieted, she spends a desultory day doing as her mother enjoined her, playing music. The melodies are tinged with a sadness she cannot explain and hearers daydream of minutes of loss, the private moments when they realised their life would not always be as they once wanted it to have been, or they broke a toy, or grew out of games they once loved to play; they feel sad as they pass.

At the end of the day she decides it is time to find company and heads to the *King Street*, where tonight there is music.

Riley is there. He has his prized red Gibson Les Paul slung over his shoulder and a group of cronies gathered in front of him as he plays. The noise he makes, well-worn blues licks, the predictable *chunder chunder* of the chord sequence is so loud it makes her want to vomit. Riley struts with his red guitar, imagining he is a rock god. He eyes her in the crowd, assessing her looks, her clothes – he has had a victory over her, though she doesn't know it. That little fool who thought he could be her friend, he has put that to an end.

She sees him, reads an expression of gloating in him, and loathing ignites in her.

Later in the evening, the MC asks her to play. A group of musicians and admirers demand the same, but she holds back. The night proceeds, with Riley insisting on playing behind other singers, stealing the life from their tunes with his ego.

Still the night draws on, and Donitza does not play. Until, when Riley is away from the amps, she stands on a tall stool by the bar and starts a mazurka. A melody that begins with a single spark, slowly and sadly, then feeds upon itself and grows. A simple rhythm at first, that doubles back on itself and accelerates like a sled down a slope, bumping along, careering forwards, taking the room, the pub, the people with it. The sound is all acoustic, and someone at the back starts to clap along with her, making the pub erupt with an ever-intensifying rhythm, with shouts and joy and a staccato of laughter.

The sinuous notes build their harmonies more until the music becomes something entirely its own. There is yet more power growing in the melody, so that it buds a second melody that emerges in the spaces between the notes of the first. The rhythm builds stronger still, and it feels as if the two melodies are counterbalanced against each other – one strong and powerful, the other something flexible and soft that wraps itself in the empty spaces of the first. Sometimes the first melody drops away completely, and the second comes up stronger, sometimes the first is the stronger and the second a counterpoint to it.

The music grows wilder and faster, and the revellers feel a sense of delirium rise up in themselves. It is something like a spell – the power of the moment creating intense feelings that sweep the crowd along. There is uproar now, as the magic works its way into their minds, and when Riley comes back to the room, he is astonished to see an animated crowd, and her, the Snow Witch, standing on a bar-room stool, ascendant above people transformed into rhythm incarnate. *Who is she?* He curses her under his breath and plugs his guitar into his amp. But the landlord pulls the plug on him before he can start, so he is forced to watch her move the crowd in a way he never has and never will, doing something he does not understand. Giving to them. Giving to them the sounds they need to hear and lifting them on a wave.

That witch. He hisses the words under his breath as he watches her, standing triumphant on her bar stool, the crowd going crazy around her – the room even seeming to grow brighter. Brighter than it was when he was playing, for sure. Finally, he gives in, moving closer, watching her in that wool dress, seeing the hint of her body through the holes in the knit, desiring her more, until at last, positioned near her, he puts out an unseen foot and trips one of the dancers, who jolts and tumbles into her stool.

The spell is broken. The dancers straighten as the magic drains from them. The violinist throws her arms up as she topples backward in a vain effort to regain her balance; steadily overending like a young tree felled. She lands, with a *crunch* and *crash*, as the violin cracks under the impact, smashing with a gut-wrenching sound.

There is silence for a moment. Then a wailing, keening shout, like the scream of a person dying, rises through the room.

Donitza is on the floor, shrieking with the pent-up pain of her short-but-oh-so-long life as she stares desperation at the violin – before she curls in a ball, her arms pulled in close in front of her, her hands over her eyes.

Silent.

*

That night, the inhabitants at the edge of the frozen lake wake to an otherworldly noise. The banker in the big villa looks to his wife, who sits blinking into the newly-sparked lamplight. The inhabitants of the 1920s Deco apartment block overlooking it peer from their windows, screwing their eyes to see, while a line of people pushes through the snow, some in Wellington boots pulled on over nightclothes, crocodiling down to the lake. There they stand and lift their mobile phones to record the phenomenon. *Boom!* The sound resounds across the snow-smothered island. *Boom!* The ice has set completely solid, its full thickness expanding out and pushing against the pleasure lake's banks. *Boom!* A deep, thunderous crack that almost deafens with its eerie echoes, juddering through the ice. It is the most extraordinary thing. The pedalo swans huddled at the lake's centre vibrate in a ring of plastic, frozen whiteness.

A seven-year-old girl who has followed her daddy down to the lake, a mop of curls and ugly glasses and who has been reading her bible tells her daddy:

"It is the devil, Papa, trying to get out from below."

Part 2

ONE cold morning Donitza saw the Red Man at her mother's window. He stared in through the glass and she screamed, bringing her mother running from the back garden where she had been staring down with growing horror at the column of smoke rising from the valley floor. His face was a shimmering scarlet ball.

Her mother hesitated for a moment then leapt forward as he tried to open the front door. She caught the rough-hewn handle in both hands and pushed her weight against it. With a stern look she ordered her daughter: "The bag I told you to get ready. Get it. We're leaving. Put on some extra warm clothing, too, Little Sparrow, it's so cold out there. And bring your violin." Then, as Donitza scurried to her bedroom, her mother released the door and the Red Man fell into the house.

Donitza heard the heated exchange between them while she scrabbled around in the bedroom for her bag, the man shouting that the Wolves had devoured the village and now they were coming here. He spoke of his wife and children, then broke down and wept in great, deep sobs. Her mother spoke kind words, calming words that after a while made the sobbing subside. When Donitza emerged from her room, carrying a cloth bag adorned with green leaves on a blue background, he was sitting quietly with tears in his eyes as her mother washed the wound on his brow.

A bullet from the Wolves – the Wolf Militia – had grazed his scalp all along the forehead and he was saying quietly that God had saved him. This God, Donitza supposed, was the Potter her mother had mentioned who had made the first man from red clay.

After the wound was dressed, he invited Donitza to kneel with him and give thanks for their deliverance, but her mother snapped at him that now was not the time - instead they should be on their ways. Still he insisted that they pray together, burying his bandaged head and bearded face in his hands. Her mother, furious, ran from the room to gather her things saying to a mystified Donitza, "Do you see the madness in these people?"

While he was still praying, her mother took his shoulders between her hands and shook him roughly, announcing loudly: "Now we must go. There are paths through the woods that will take us to safety."

Eventually, after what seemed like an age, the man stood up, fortified and strengthened by the moments he had taken to commune with his Creator. In a calm voice he said, "I will go first to make sure it is safe for you women." Ignoring her mother's warning, he threw the door open and stepped out on to the snow. He took two steps forward and a hole opened in the back of his head, his blood and brains exploding backwards, spattering the opposite wall of the room.

Donitza thought with an air of unreality that this God of his was an indecisive one.

Her mother meanwhile was cursing herself: "How did I not sense this would come today? How did I not know?"

She turned to her daughter, her face stone-hard. "We must go another way," she said, and clutching her daughter's hand tight in hers made for the back door.

Donitza sees them now as if she is looking back over her shoulder through the front window again: the men emerging from the woods where she once played, moving toward the house, stepping quickly yet cautiously, in the mountain green of the militia, each carrying a Kalashnikov, each wearing black boots and heavy coats, their breaths steaming against the mountain air. Behind them, in the distance, she can hear the sound of a helicopter rising like a deadly insect. Close to hand, steam and the smell of excrement are rising from the corpse of the Red Man who is redder now even than he was when Donitza first saw him.

She dives through the back door, over the herb patch, the chickens flurrying up with panicked complaint, a scrabble across the snow, her violin case banging against her knees as she pants and slips on rock and ice. They make their ways between trees that line a path along the edge of the escarpment until the way bends up and meets with the road. Her mother looks carefully for movement, then steps out. Donitza follows her – running on to the road – a stonestudded mud track with ruts coated in ice. She pants relief as they arrive at its far side where the cover of the forest awaits.

Faces appear. Emerging from the darkness. Faces that look on them with soulless eyes.

One of them gestures the pair to stop and then the men approach the woman and her daughter, guns raised.

Donitza pushes into her mother's skirts while around them stone-faced soldiers look on, smoking and coughing in the winter air.

A man pushes through the group, their Captain. An ugly man with a black beard and dark eyes beneath a bush of matted hair surmounted by a green cap that looks as if he is about to play baseball with an American team. His lips, she notices, are fat and pink and he wears a stud in his left ear that glimmers incongruously in the winter light. She is shivering as she swings her violin case forlornly around her knees. Behind the soldiers, a lorry pulls up and thirty people, ashen-faced, are roughly pushed from it.

Her mother eyes the Captain with a level look.

"I don't know what you are doing here, but we live away from the village. We have nothing to do with your war here."

The Captain studies her, taking her in appreciatively. He glances down at Donitza and gives her a slow, thoughtful smile, then pulls out a packet of raisins. He takes one and drops it in his mouth, chewing absently.

"Trying to give up cigarettes," he explains lightly, before waiting a moment in the icy air to answer offhandedly. "This is all routine. Don't let it worry you."

Her mother relaxes, the tension dropping from her shoulders as she exhales a sigh.

"I, I thought..." she looks past him. The people from the village are being walked to the road's edge which runs beside a dizzying drop to a brake of pines 300 metres below. The canopy down there is layered with picturesque white-rimed pine needles, the whole supported on straight poles of elephant-wrinkled bark. It looks like frozen clouds.

"What are you doing with them?" she asks.

There are men and women, all shapes and sizes, tall and small, fat, thin, balding, grey, young. Each a life, each a history, each the current manifestation of a line of loves and minglings and accidents and friendships. The summation of an infinite series of beliefs, tears and sunshine. Each now shivers in the cold on the edge of a mountain.

He turns and waves his hand. "With them? Oh, it's all routine." He squats down, haunches on heels, and looks at Donitza on the level. He smiles again and offers her the box of raisins.

"Go on, take it," he says.

After a pat on the shoulder from her mother, she accepts it and tastes the sweet wrinkled flesh in her mouth. She smiles, shyly.

"Do you play this?" he asks, pointing at the violin case.

She nods.

"Are you good?"

She nods again.

Behind him, a soldier puts the barrel of his gun against the temple of a young man and pulls the trigger. With an echoing *crack* and an explosion of colour, the young man's arms go limp at his side as his body crumples backwards and he disappears from the roadside into the empty air. The woman who is next in line starts to shake, looking around her for anything that might offer a lifeline. A puddle forms at her feet.

Donitza's mother takes hold of her daughter's shoulders and grips them so hard her fingers hurt where they dig in.

"You said –"

"Yes, it is all routine," he answers. "I heard what you said, that you have nothing to do with the town. And yet, you were giving shelter to someone here." He points at the crumpled body outside the doorway, a red gash on the snow. "Someone we would say is not one of us."

"He just came here, I didn't even know his name."

The Captain shrugs. "This is unfortunate for you. But it is my task to cleanse this area of those who are not with us. You see, you are either with us, or you are against us."

Behind the Captain, the young soldier puts his hand on the frightened woman's shoulder in a calming way. She looks to him with relief. He smiles and very gently pushes her backwards. She teeters on the edge for a split second, her arms spinning to find her balance and then she vanishes. She makes no sound, as if she is too frightened to accuse her killer of her murder.

The Captain considers her mother a while longer. "You say you had nothing to do with the village, in either community. So, while you may not be against us, you are not one who can be said to be with us."

"No, but listen – "

"Your daughter will play for you," he says, an amused light in his eyes. "She will play for all of us."

The image collapses under the agony of remembrance. Donitza's mind is a jumble of recollections. A kaleidoscope of tumbling scenes: a lost young man in a red hat, the streets of the island city, her mother, the flowers and plants of childhood, Victorian tiles glistening outside an English pub, a tank rumbling on caterpillar tracks in the distance. Everything is jumbled and caught in a circling nightmare of images and sounds.

Snow falls.

She sobs at this blizzard of remembrances that shows no sign of resolving into a shape she can understand or bear. Just more images and more memories of a life she does not want to have lived nor has the power to understand. She is an animal, aware of scents and the movement of the air and the shapes of the woods and mountains, the flight of birds and the growth of flowers, daisies spreading their faces to the sun, dandelions seeding skyward in the summer air, the fall of rain that laughs on the leaves, the balm-bearing wind that comes from the south and the strife-laden storm from the north.

A gentle hand rests on her brow for a few seconds and she blinks up at Celia gazing down at her.

"There, there," she says. "Are you all right, dearie? All right now?"

Donitza looks at her in silence, her hazel eyes dark contracted points, jet or obsidian or the ebony of her violin's fingerboard.

She sits urgently. "Where is my violin? Where is it?"

"Hang on, dearie, I'll get it."

Celia brings the case over and lays it on the bed. Donitza looks a question at her. Did she dream it? The memory of last night is a blur. A bad dream? An evil spirit that took on the semblance of reality but lived only in her mind? A bubble of hope rises, and she opens the case, hands shaking.

She blinks as the bubble bursts. Grief snatches her up into its cruel arms. She is a child, lost in the woods, the world exploding around her.

Can her fingers cry as well?

At the place where the neck joins the body, the soundboard is stoved in where the neck has pulled away. *Broken!* Cracked open with a deep wound that can't be repaired.

Before Celia can think of any words to comfort her, the doorbell rings. The old lady dithers a moment, unsure what to do, until another ring clatters through the house and with Pavlovian obedience she heads downstairs to answer it.

*

It was obvious, Riley thinks, *As soon as I saw where they brought her. The dress, the clothes. Obvious.*

As he stands in the snow, he recalls with some pleasure how the foreign bitch was sobbing as he'd watched from the other side of the street as friends delivered her to the door. To think: she had tried to blank him, to refuse to acknowledge his presence, in his patch, on his island, his manor. Last night, there she was, laid low by a neatly placed boot and a gentle shove. *Well, I got a reaction from her, at last!*

He is all bravado now, the imaginings that there was something *other* about her gone in the daylight and the drama of the night before. Her sobbing. He'd found it vaguely revolting. For what? A violin. A piece of wood and glue and bone and metal. *Funny to see her laid low by something so inconsequential.* This thought had first come to him the previous night as he headed back to crash at Vee's, while her two fat children whose names he couldn't remember lay wakeful and afraid in the next room. *But there it is.*

That night he'd stared into the half-dark after roughly screwing Vee, who wordlessly turned her back to him, and he'd wondered how this Eastern woman would react – how grateful she would be – were he to bring her another violin. He would, as he always did with the women he wanted, exploit her weakness to draw her to him.

That's why this morning he'd wandered along to the second-hand shops; in that part of the city the streets resembled a frontier town with their Victorian buildings jutting over plastic shop frontages, like the upper half of a Wild West film set. Those old edifices were covered in snow and cold and accusation.

One antiques shop was stuffed to the ceiling with furniture. Victorian high back chairs, magazines, posters, ships in bottles, clocks, paintings, tobacco pipes, jewellery, coronation tins and naval uniforms. The discards of previous lives awaiting reincarnation.

Exploring under a table, he'd found on the floor a black, hard case and pulled it out to inspect. A violin in medium brown, heavily varnished. A haggle ensued, followed by an offer of a few pounds – and then it was his.

So, here he is again. After knocking at the same door he'd watched he enter the previous night, he stands in silent expectation. His prey lies upstairs, paralysed by her disaster. He senses it. He senses her helplessness. *An instinct.* The same instinct detected that Vee, so desperate for human touch, would let him treat her as he does. It vibrates in him as he pictures Donitza prone in her bed, or perhaps sniffs the despair wafting down the stairs into the hallway when Celia opens the door and stands searching her memory for a second, before saying:

"James. James Riley?"

Today has been a trying day for the old woman. The strain at her guest's distress shows on her face.

"Hello Mrs Downey," he replies with a smile that leaves his eyes untouched.

Bizarrely, he feels young again and has to steady himself in a headlong rush of memories and emotions before reminding himself he is not a nine-year-old.

"I've brought something for your lodger," he says. "Tell her it's from me."

Celia looks him in the face and doesn't know what to make of him or his gift. It has been a long time since she saw him run up and down this road as a boy. But with the ray of light that shines within her, the switch trips in her mind and she sees the good in this visit. She remembers him playing with others on this very road – a football through a window, his mother apologising to a neighbour, James looking on, unreadable in his expression, but chastened by the threat of withheld pocket money.

"Thank you James. That is very kind."

As he walks away, Riley wonders about her words. "Kind." It is not a word he associates with himself. "Kind." It makes him think for a moment of other possibilities. Of another James, his mother's son, who grew up thinking of others, grew up to be a nice respectable middle class boy, a pillar of the community.

It is such an alien thought that it amuses him. In his mind, he sees this other James dispensing kindnesses to the poor, attending church, working with the homeless, giving them soup in the freezing air. He builds the image brighter and bigger, and adds more extremeness. Helping old ladies across the road, organizing a gang of schoolchildren to do kindnesses to the aged, being fêted on the streets so that the city's moron populace kisses the ground upon which he walks. He pictures himself a saviour of mankind, quickening people to life with his touch. They leap from their graves singing "Hallelujah!" All to follow him. To follow him and – as is the point of religion – to tell him how wonderful he is.

He laughs at the vanity of the old woman in seeing herself in him. "Kind." He mimics the word, speaking in a mock-feeble parody of a woman's voice. "Kind." And he spits into the snow another ball of yellow phlegm, as if needing to expel the word from his mouth.

*

Donitza, meanwhile, is paralysed by images of her past.

On the high mountain road, her mother grips her daughter's right arm, looks long into her face, her eyes projecting – *love – desperation – reassurance* – a progression of emotions Donitza reads in in her face.

"You will play, my Little Flower, my Sparrow," she tells her daughter, her voice uneven, struggling for measure, running her hand softly through the girl's dark hair.

"Remember my lessons. Euterpe is the name of the presiding power over you, in one old tongue. She has other names. Remember she holds you in her protection. Now play, my love."

She hugs her daughter close, then lays her hands on her shoulders and gives an imploring smile. "Play something beautiful. Promise me you will play for your protection?"

"I promise, mother."

"Good, my Flower."

The Captain grips her mother's arm and she stands, searching for the soul behind his eyes, weighing whether to obey. She submits and with a haunting look, a tender, sad smile, conjures every kiss, every moment of laughter, every lesson she has taught her. She walks backward for three steps, then quickly turns. But Donitza sees the tears, and fear tightens her body.

With scientific interest, the Captain looks from the mother's face to the dark-haired girl's, wondering how she will respond.

"Play," he says quietly, a short soft syllable. Two guards walk her mother to the edge of the road, where the beautiful white valley stretches away beneath a dizzying drop.

"Play."

*

Riley steps into Vee's house and bangs his snowbound boots on the wall. Vee feels her heart flutter with a rush of adrenalin. He is back again. Back again and in her house; back with her and her two boys, Daryl and Jord. She feels relief and anticipation, like she does at the unwinding of a cocaine wrap

From her narrow perspective, her mind burdened with dark thoughts and the chemical interference of dope, amphetamines and fluoxetine, she sometimes senses a glimmer, as if the cloud has lifted from her life and she walks through an upland filled with sunlight where she and James are together and happy. It is an idyll drawn from kids' cartoons and colouring-in books – the outlined image of a farmer and his wife with a cow, drawn by the simple sweep of a pen in a handful of lines curved enough to denote "friendly" to a child. This she supposes is what "happy" points to.

Vee. Little Vee. Vicky. Victoria. She has lived an avalanche of a life since she slipped from the high ledge of the familial home at 14 into an abusive relationship, through pregnancy and unwilling abortion to care homes and one night stands, finally to two completed terms. Her life is summed up on social worker's files in words such as *instability, confusion* and *vulnerable*, all of which point toward a State-assisted life.

But the State, her great enabler, has been there for her in the place of her disapproving parents in only a limited way. The smile she met on Christmas Day the first year she ran away from home came from a carpet salesman in the full stampede of a midlife crisis destined to do time for overliking minors. The hand on her brow when she overdosed on heroin at 16 was a paramedic's. The State has prescribed her anti-depressants and enough hours in the vacuum of the day to wreck her life in relative comfort. She sprawls on her sofa like a broken starfish washed up on the beach, during a lull in the storm that is her life, bedraggled and lost, and with no way back to the water.

She is conscious of none of this view of her life, and dreams of happiness. But Vee doesn't know happiness. She knows Riley.

In the doorway he shouts to her to make him a cup of tea and she, grateful for a purpose, drags herself off the sofa and pads to the kitchen to put the kettle on, hugging to her body her once-white dressing gown. *Calm him down, manage him. He'll be good.* She just needs a bit of a smile, a kindness from him, those revivifying moments that she doesn't realise come deliberately between his deftly administered cruelty, feeding her a dose of enough non-pain to keep her hungry for more. That after all is the meaning of *Treat them mean, keep them keen,* which could be part of Riley's catechism if he had one. Or cataclysm.

He is seated on the sofa, brooding over something when she comes back to the room and hands him his cup from nailbitten hands. He is channel-hacking on her freeview box, looking for something banal enough to stay with when squeals of laughter come from Jord and Daryl in their room upstairs. A few minutes later and another cascade of joy sees him tense like iron under load, then sink into the sofa further, seeking to lose himself in the dullness of a programme on the chemtrail conspiracy interspersed with adverts for winter sun breaks. *Did we know the world is controlled by mind-control drugs sprayed from the wings of passenger jets, - oh and would you like to escape to exotic Thailand in one of them?*

After handing over the violin and hearing the old woman's misplaced appreciation, his mind reacted by looping backward to something far darker. A mood has settled on him. An impulse to do bad things. As if it somehow validates him and disproves the old woman. An image plays in his mind. In slow motion, the long-haired girl falling backwards, tumbling through the air, her hands raised upwards. *What is this?* He can't get it out of his mind. Over and over the same movie. *Again. Again.* An emotion of self-loathing goes with it. *The fall.* And again. *The fall, backwards, arms feeling for something to grasp. Something.* And each time the darkness rises like a tide. *The sea. The black, black sea.* He needs to do something to blank this. The image. *Again. Again.*

A further burst of laughter from their room is enough, and to a concerned shout of "Jim!" from Vee, Riley leaps up and thumps upstairs like a panther, his body all power and anger.

He comes to the doorway to see the two boys doubled with giggles as two plastic balls propel themselves across the floor. Riley looks on as the pair of balls bang into each other and bounce off again, two small creatures seeking each other inside, one ball made of blue translucent plastic, the other of yellow.

Two rodents. Their pets in the hamster balls their mother bought them in a rare moment of decisiveness. They had begged her for those hamsters, the cage, the straw, the feed. She had said no. But a schoolfriend's dad had given them the secondhand cage and the boys had amassed the rest with the instinct of scavengers and the resourcefulness of beggars until at last their mother had given in and bought the creatures. The golden-brown one Daryl called *The Dalek*, the other, dark brown with white spots under its cheeks and a white spot on its back, Jord called *John Wesley*. It was a name Jord had liked for no other reason than it sounded funny. And so, at

Christmas, this present had arrived from Vee – a pair of hamster balls for the gentle creatures to test their freedom without getting lost or mauled by neighbourhood cats.

Riley watches them rocking across the floor, the creatures inside like the tank commanders of a kitsch-futuristic weapon of war seeming to doggy-paddle the air. It is funny. He can see that. He can see that the boys are loving this, and what that means. A link to Vee, an unplugged emotional window that enables them to connect to her and take her for just a brief moment out of his control. He hates these little shits with their pink allergenic burger-additive skin and the excess of fat that softens their profiles to marshmallow. He hates the threat they present to his domination of her. How much more under his control would she be, he wonders, how much more isolated were these two little piggies dead?

With deliberate irony he knocks on the door, creasing a faux smile. They look up together and their pinkness goes pinker as the skin beneath their eyes sinks in a frozen moment of hate.

"Knock, knock," Riley says to the silent room, as the two balls continue careering around it. "Am I interrupting?"

The boys say nothing, kneeling on the floor looking up at him, frozen in the moment. The Dalek's blue ball bumps against his feet, the snout quivering as it tests the air. In its rodent consciousness it smells something it finds uninteresting and the boys watch as the ball turns away and starts to rock in the other direction.

With a deft movement Riley lifts the ball and unscrews it, dropping the parts on the floor as he lifts the hamster by the tail, its paws scrabbling the air as it inverts, bending its neck back vainly to find the horizontal. The boys squeal with their highpitched voices. This pleases him.

"Ah, look at him," he says with mock appreciation. "He likes being out and about. An adventurer."

"Please, put him down," Daryl whimpers with soft desperation. "Please."

Riley savours the moment, lifting the struggling creature in front of his face and opening his mouth as if to eat it. The boys scream again. "No!"

Riley laughs, a sensation he experiences only rarely and he swells with the power he feels. These little lives, they please him when they are in anguish, at least.

"He's a character isn't he?" he says. "Driving around in his ball like that. I bet he likes to go to the funfair. I bet he does."

He chooses the place carefully. Often enough he's heard the boys beg their mother to take them to the western pier, that stunted platform on the seafront that juts bestilted over the sea, facing the shipping lanes that run through the harbour mouth. An image of summer days and the boys spinning on the Waltzer, puking chips and Tango – and loving every minute of it. The funfair: he's heard them talk of it with joy and desire and laughter.

Perfect.

"We could take him on a ride. Shall we put him on the funfair ride?"

Daryl sums up the courage to answer back. "He doesn't like funfairs," he says. "He wants to stay at home."

Unable and unwilling to restrain himself at the contradiction, Riley shouts down at the boy, each syllable landing like a punch. "Don't you ever tell me you know different. I know all about everything. Get it?" He grabs a long football sock hung over the end of a bunk bed and stuffs the hamster in. "Let's give him a ride!"

He takes hold of the end of the sock and starts to spin it, the weight of the hamster's body tumbling downwards into the heel as the acceleration builds. The boys are going crazy, standing up to catch the sock while Riley laughs and shouts, lifting the spinning weight above his head and whirling it like a rotor blade. "He likes a ride, see? He loves it!"

Daryl finds his anger and punches Riley in the stomach. A pathetic strengthless impact against his darkly unbending torso. But

Riley is surprised by the petty rebellion and grows more angry, spinning the sock faster and faster, the tight bundle at its base unmoving as it presses centrifugally against the fabric, and Daryl pummels ineffectually at his trunk.

"You bastard," Daryl shouts. "Leave him alone. Put him down. You fucking bastard."

"What?" Riley leans over him, pole-axing the boy with a syllable. Daryl scrabbles on the floor in hysteria, his hands over his head, sobbing.

Riley, satisfied, slows the spin. *That'll do. Little shits,* he thinks to himself. He still has the spin going and turns to leave. Then he sees that Vee is watching him, helpless. Hopeless.

"James," she says. "Please."

That's enough for him. With a final thrust he slams the ball of the sock into the wall. A smear of blood appears over the light switch.

He looks at it and catches a sight of himself in a mirror in the toilet across the landing. He inhales as he looks at the man staring back, emotionless, cold – moving in a world in which there are no people, but things.

Something has changed in him. He can't identify what exactly, but it is something to do with the Witch. The fall. The backwards fall. Is this a kind of desperation? Against breaking something beautiful he pits his belief that he is born to destroy. It is this that makes him who he is.

He leaves the house, a wash of black meaninglessness pulsing through him. His life is a well with no bottom, or the seabed at night. Cold. Alone. He imagines himself as if wrapped in a bag, chained, sinking. *The sea. The black, black sea.* He feels the water closing over him so that he becomes at last only dark intention moving without purpose and without hope through noiseless night.

*

For Donitza, it is as if she has vanished from the present day and is living solely in the past that she ran from for so long. She feels it, sees it, hears it. Everything that once happened is happening again. Every detail of that day.

The girl Donitza shivers. She feels the cold air whip around her, but she is not sure whether it is cold or fear that raises her goosebumps and makes her shake.

As the Captain looks on, Donitza's fingers struggle to grip the strings. She fingers a few notes without bowing them, uncertain what to play. She senses that he is losing patience, and fears what that might mean for her and her mother. She must impress him. She must play. Euterpe will protect her if she plays.

She bows a note, her mind not knowing where she will go with this, her heart shrinking in her as the first note sounds. Another follows, one tone up, held long and sonorously in the mountain air. A higher note, a natural seventh from the first is followed by a fourth below the starting note, a tone higher and then a drop by a fifth. These are the details she remembers, before the melody takes flight with a life of its own.

The tune Donitza plays is a sad one. Filled with low sonorous notes, it circles around like a creature lost, sniffing at the roots of trees to find a direction; not knowing where it might find shelter. The melody cycles in this way, speaking of loss and hardship and hopeless nights of loneliness when a man may look into himself and see only unfathomable darkness reflected in the mirror of his soul. A sad tune, desolate and horrifying.

The Captain looks at the girl as she plays, surprised by the sureness of the performance even in this glacial air where his butcher's hands are only ever warmed by the blood of his victims. A shot rings out behind him and another figure – that of an old heavy-jowled man in a dark blue overcoat vanishes into the blue sky. Donitza's body jolts, but she plays on.

The Captain turns, annoyed at the interruption and gestures his men to stop what they are doing for a moment as the melody travels onward. Now the notes speak of a lost beast seeking refuge, seeking a home, a haven, lamenting what it does not have, an edge of anger in its feral sinews.

Donitza's eyes cloud to sightlessness. She has never played like this. She feels not-present, a being composed of sound entirely. Vibration with no substance, a wind that blows on the strings. She is air, a shadow, a mist, a movement glimpsed in the corner of her own eye, a light on the water, a scent dimly remembered of woodsmoke, a plume that rises and blows away. She cannot explain it in other ways. Another mind has taken hold of her.

She has a vision, or a sentiment that makes sense to her at that moment. She feels the magic circle and sees the hub of the world, the axle around which everything spins, strike down through her. She sees, as if in a dream, these men watching her as they stand on the edge of the wheel, peering in from the rim, distant, unable to touch her.

The melody changes with a subtle shift. It takes a direction. The lost creature begins a trek across the snows, a flight from somewhere to somewhere, it doesn't know where. It comes to an area on the edge of a scarp that thickens with trees. Birds flutter in the spring air and with their cries manufacture the golden light of day. They are startled by the creature's presence. It hears the laughter of water. A stream. The lost creature follows it for a while, till it basks in the sunlight a moment, its savagery drowsing in radiant warmth.

Now it follows the river further, down to richer pastures and a valley. There are watchful men here who move with guns. The creature slinks stealthily in the night and under the light of the full moon at last realises its true nature. It is possessed by the power of the pale light. It is the Destroyer. It is the Ravager.

Ahead of it shifts a herd of goats, grey and black in the white moonlight – they look upon the creature with eyes ancient as the night. The moonlight finds them, picks them out in hunting light. The killing moon watches as the creature pounces, wild with rage, deliriously ecstatic as it tears and destroys.

The goat it traps in its maw weakens in its struggle and collapses. The wolf creature – for now we can see what it is at last – rips it, devours it.

The night passes.

The next day, in the light, a man lies naked in a brake of trees in the mountains. Outside a house, a shirt and trousers are drying on a line. He steals them and goes on, deeper into the world of men, afraid of what will happen when the next moon comes. He lives among the unsuspecting populace waiting to inhabit again a body of destructive force.

Sometimes, he grows hungry at the thought of the killing he will do.

One night, transformed by the moon, the creature wanders savage in a wood seeking a new kill. It comes to a house among the trees where a woman sits by a fire. It will strike, kill, destroy. Rage rushes through its head, a red cloud of annihilation that will conquer everything. It watches from the eaves, ready to strike.

Then the woman sings an old song that speaks to its heart and, not knowing how or why, the creature pads forward, its head lowered. It bows before the woman, who speaks in a soft voice, her face flickering in the firelight. She says:

"I am your friend."

And so the melody ends and the Captain is silent for a time that seems to stretch on, unendurably long. The girl Donitza, perceptive with the light of inspiration, senses an emotion in his heart as of a scale in the balance. He is surprised by the performance, she senses a stirring in him that he does not recognise.

The soldiers stand nearby awaiting his orders. Their exact positions are seared into Donitza's mind. Every needle on every tree, the way the snow is piled in crystal colonies, the men waiting for the word from their Captain. All of this is photographed by her memory.

The Captain smiles down to her, absent for a few seconds. In her heightened state, she thinks she can read his thoughts. A flash of images from his mind.

He is remembering a visit he once paid with his mother when he was a boy to one of his country's tourist regions. There, as they see a swan on the water, they have one of their few moments of intimacy. His mother digs into her memory to find something to tell him as they are rowed quietly across the lake, the reflection of a red and white brick tower distorting in the water, the dip of oars from the oarsman sending out ripples to the swan swimming a few yards off. His mothers tells him of the idea of the swan song.

"At the point of its death, the swan keens with the most beautiful sound. A sound so unlike its normal voice. They say it is unbearable in its beauty... It's a story I heard from my mother when I was young." She shrugs when she sees her son does not respond to her words. She exhales a nervous half laugh. "It is ridiculous, of course."

But he likes the idea. There is a romance to it.

Later in life he sees the idea for what it really signifies – that you allow someone to soar at the moment before they are crushed. Perhaps then, if you are lucky, you might see someone at their best before they die. It is a prospect that both excites him and gives him a sense of the justness of his murders. For no-one is ever good enough.

The girl understands this even as her insight begins to fade.

Now, looking down on Donitza, the Captain waits a while longer for the scales to tip in his heart the way they always tip. Donitza feels a crushing sense of powerlessness, freezing to the spot as he weighs her.

Her mother looks on from the road's edge with tears in her eyes. The Captain waves a hand carelessly. A young man steps forward and puts a hand on her shoulder –

One minute she is there, the next she has stepped backward and is gone.

"Mama!" Donitza shouts, the horror in her voice accompanied by a streaking flash of light. The Captain pulls a pistol and points it at her head. As he does so, the army truck disintegrates in flames and the earth shakes. There is a rush of fire and another explosion destroys an armoured car along the road in a maelstrom of flame.

Donitza falls to the ground as the Captain cranes up at the sky. The bullet he fires passes over her. Militia and civilians scatter beneath the deafening roar of a jet.

She lies there for a moment, breathing raggedly, wide-eyed in shock, then runs to the wood's dark edge.

She is blind with tears as she breaks into the ferns and the tang-resined pungency of the woods, its browned needle-carpet springy where the snow has not reached.

The rich sap of the pinewood fills her nose with sharpness, even through streaming mucus and tears.

*

She is woken from the nightmare by a sound. Celia is at the door to her room again. She is holding something in her hands.

"I don't know what to make of this," she says. "A delivery."

"What delivery?"

"This!" she says, and shows her a violin case, then hands it over as Donitza sits up and stretches out her arms.

With urgent fingers, Donitza throws open the case and gasps. She pulls the instrument out and examines it. Something flutters inside her for a brief moment.

Just a cheap violin, but to think – it is a kindness, and she recognises that intention.

"Who would do this?" she asks aloud, already knowing the answer.

"It was from..."

"I know, I know," she says, raising her hand. She looks at it a moment. "I want to talk to him."

In a snowstorm of thoughts and feelings, she throws back the bedclothes. This act of kindness, it will be acknowledged. A glimmer of something bright shines in her – a connection that allows for new possibilities, that disproves her history. She will grasp it this time, she will acknowledge it in the way that last time she did not. *There is kindness*, she tells herself when she thinks of Celia and Eddy. There is a reality in which people care. In such thoughts she suspects lies her salvation.

*

Before she leaves the house, she steps to the back door and opens it on to the garden. The air has gathered in a vortex at the side of the house and she lets an icecold blast gyre into the kitchen like an evil spirit.

She ignores the cold in favour of an idea that she does not fully recognise. It is not a familiar feeling, but she can sense it moving in herself. The emotion brings fresh interpretation to actions and moments in her past whose meaning teetered in her mind, a bar on a pivot that might tip one way or another. *The fox.* She has a sudden understanding that her treatment of it over the last few weeks stands for kindness and that is why it is important to her. She was not sure. She fed it from instinct when she first saw it – to placate it in case it tried to do her harm, to lead her astray – but now she realises –

"I *am* your friend," she says to the cold air, pulling the bacon from the packet she has taken from the fridge with a warmness of heart.

The fox is somewhere out there, in the bushes, lingering, watching. She feels its green eyes on her. She sings in a low voice and it comes forward, its head bowed yet eager, and she feeds the scrap to it from her fingers. Its soft tongue is warm and wet on her palm as it takes the meat with exquisite delicacy and leaves the remembrance of a breath on her hand.

When it is done, she steps back inside and leaves through the front door, pushing through the snow, again with that subtle glimmer of hope inside her that comes from the power of connection.

She goes down past the cake shop with its icing fantasies in the window, looking around her as if the whole world has been covered by a mad sugar chef. She goes past the putting green skirting the beach where pebbledashed snowmen have rolled into existence, and continues on breathlessly to the fort.

She comes to the iron door and bangs on it, calling. "Eddy! Eddy! Let me in."

No sound comes from within and she waits a moment, a sense of foreboding growing inside her. She bangs on the door again, *clang clang clang*, and waits a while longer. She hears a movement inside.

"Eddy, that's you! I can hear you! I want to thank you for the violin!"

A step. Breathing on the far side of the door, close to her ear, a rasping sound.

"Go away! Leave me alone."

"But I want to thank you."

"I didn't give you anything. Go. Go away! Leave me alone. I don't want to see you."

He adds these last words with an angry force in his voice that bowls Donitza back on her heels.

"Eddy! What's wrong? Eddy?"

There is a long pause.

"Go. Go away. Never come back."

She senses that the presence has gone and she turns in the snow, doubly downcast, the hope that briefly flowered in her crushed. She sinks. Darkness pushes in at the edge of her field of vision.

Along with the darkness there is not only a feeling of betrayal, but also of puzzlement.

Puzzlement at the gift.

*

After the werewolf left the mother and daughter sitting by the fire and vanished back into the woods, the night sky bent over them to listen more closely to her mother's words.

"Wolves themselves are not evil creatures," her mother told her.

"Oh! Listen to me," she added with an ironic smile. "*Evil!* How easy it is to slip into these words that are black and white words! Such words are words for men. Wolves are what they are – creatures of nature who hunt in packs and revere the moon. This is their nature. Nature herself is a principle that shifts, like light and shade or fire and heat. Always shifting, always moving."

Her daughter looked to her, seeing the yellow firelight dance on her skin as she admired her severe beauty. Her mother added:

"Animals are our friends most of the time. Or at least, our allies. In most cases, they understand us and we understand them – even if they are bewitched a while with moon madness."

She reached out her hand and drew her daughter toward her, Donitza feeling the strong suppleness of her mother's hands closing around her arm. Her mother ran her fingers through her daughter's hair, clearing the strands from her eyes and then kissing her forehead.

"But there is one animal you must look out for. He is the wolf in man's skin. The wolf in man's skin is caught half way between animal and man and is trapped there. For him, there is no transformation. He appears to be a man, but his heart is more savage than the werewolf."

Donitza looked up to her mother, seeing the play of shadows under the chin, the flicker moving lambently on the hair.

"How is he stuck, Mama?"

"He is trapped between two worlds. He cannot be our friend because he is trapped in the form of a man, and he cannot be reasoned with because his heart is that of an animal."

She took her daughter by the shoulders and looked into her eyes. "Something has happened to his soul that prevents him from completing the transformation," she said. "And lack of transformation in any case – that is death, for yourself and others. Remember that, my Sparrow."

*

In the cramped house where Vee lives with her two boys and the visiting presence of Riley, Vee is sitting, with a new thought circling in her mind –

He has changed. God, he has changed.

She can see it now. It has taken a long time, years maybe, for the illusion to fall away and for her to see Riley in the cold light of reality, whatever that is. *He's a bastard,* she thinks, because although everyone else knew it, for her this is a revelation.

In this moment of recognition, she stands as if naked before the cold light of truth, and she is afraid – afraid of the dark energy she has let into her life and the life of her boys. At first, there was nothing different in Riley from the others she let in before. He had sometimes, as others did, knocked her about. That was nothing new. But now, cleaning the mark on the wall and seeing her boys withdraw into wordless shock, this – this is something she has never known. Something new, and she fears the new most of all. There is safety in repetition, and danger in escalation. Things have got darker in a life that a long time ago ceased to be bright.

Daryl and Jord are sobbing in the wake of the murder he has wrought in their room. After she has rinsed the cloth out and put it on the radiator to dry till it becomes a hard soap-stiffened scale, she takes the sock and puts it in the bin. Daryl and Jord follow her downstairs and watch her drop it in. When she turns, they are staring at her. She reads their emotions.

"I know. I know," she says, before they speak.

"We've got to get away from him," says Jord, stating aloud what has passed between them unspoken. "Please mum, we've got to."

She comes over to them and puts her hands on their shoulders, steering them into their chaotic living room, strewn with games and DVDs and unwashed plates.

"But how do we do it?" she asks, half in desperation, half in collusion.

She likes this, she realises. She likes the feeling of closeness with them, and hopes that perhaps now she will salvage something that will mean something to them in the future – something that will pull them together as a family.

She is new to this. This kind of intimacy was not something she felt with her parents. They were strict. Her father set rules and punished with a slap from early on. And she was told from the beginning that she would be punished for being a *bad girl*, as if that was something that she was in herself rather than the creature of his judgements. Her father: on a short fuse. *The Judge.* That's how she thinks of him. He was never interested in helping her along the road of life, but only to make pronouncements about her. Her actions were a moral indicator, not a sign of the person who, with a little guidance, she might grow up to be.

And yet, there *were* times of love. There were times, she thinks, when there was happiness, and she draws on them now to talk with her kids.

"What do we do?" she asks, almost helplessly, as if she, too, is a kid again, talking about a sleeping giant and stepping carefully in its malign presence.

"We should get away," says Jord, the heavier of the two and a year older. "Just go and never come back."

Daryl, the younger one looks up with wide eyes at his mother.

"Yeah. We could get on a boat. We could go anywhere. Just away."

"Away?" she echoes the word, and sees a possibility.

Daryl is right, of course he is. There's a ferry port just down the road. *France. On the other side of the water.* She could bowl up with her two kids in St. Malo or Cherbourg and start again. Get away from all of it. From this life. From him.

A new excitement takes her.

"We can, can't we?" she says, with a breathless voice. "I could get work in a café or something. Doing English breakfasts and tea and stuff, and we'd get you to school!" This other world seems possible now. Bigger. Brighter. "Yes, that's it. We'd get you into school over there. Why not? And it'll be great. We'll just up sticks. And go. Easy."

"Yeah, mum. Yeah!" Daryl joins in, hugging her – daring to believe in this new life.

"I just need to tell him..." She grows thoughtful a moment at how that conversation would pan out. "No, maybe not tell him. Just up sticks and go. One day. When he's not looking."

She sees herself in her mind's eye: capable, living a life in France. Exotic. Otherworldly. *In France!* Smiling at the sunshine, face lifted to receive its kiss. Her boys are fit and happy, working alongside her. She is swept along with the reverie; the images rush in as she allows herself to fall in love with the dream.

"And here we are: after a few years, I'm running the café." In her imagination, the French have fallen in love with a new phenomenon – English breakfast. She's had the pain-au-chocolat and croissants from the Co-op, *there's no competition, really!* And somehow they all speak English. It's all familiar, all the same, but with an accordion soundtrack. Like a dubbed French romantic movie she saw on tv a few years back.

She talks it out, spinning a dream in the air that the boys join in building. Together, a little sundappled courtyard where the yellow patches of sunlight are moved by the trees in the wind. A rustle through the leaves. An escape like a bird in flight.

The dream tapestry grows bigger and all three of them look up at it together. She is breathless, her chest tightening, her breathing shallow.

Her eyes stay focussed on that imagined future and she rises with her boys above the misery of the now, gathering them in her arms as they move toward a perfect future, until she feels a tug pulling her back down to earth.

Fear steps in.

How to do it? What if it goes wrong? The language? What about the people? And the money? And getting away – that means passports.

In a few seconds the woven picture unravels before her, so she is left staring at its strands.

A feeling spreads through her.

Relief.

Because she knows it can't happen. Because she knows that actually, what she has with Riley, in its direction and its content, is what she has always known. That embrace: violent – maybe even deadly as it might prove to be – is the embrace of familiarity. That is enough for her. And she is sorry for the boys, but she needs this. A continuum from childhood. And besides, if she did something different from what she knows, most likely, she would find herself back in the familiar. The trap of personality.

"Where is he?" she frets, suddenly alarmed that he may not come home.

*

On Wednesday nights Celia goes to visit a friend. It is a rule. Her friend is "getting on a bit", Celia likes to say with an indulgent look on her face, confident that as long as there are "old 'uns" for her to visit on Wednesday evenings, she is not *getting on a bit*. Thus another of the self-deceptions of hope. The ritual is so important to Celia that even in the snow she goes, picking her way like a soldier through a minefield strewn with potential broken hips to stretch her leg into the back of a taxi. Today, a driver has agreed to pick her up at the end of the road, where the gritters have turned the sulphur-lamped winter into tractionable slush.

Donitza, sombre and withdrawn, offers to walk her to where the taxi's engine is puttering its vapour; nitrogen and carbon dioxide fogging into the night air. She feels she must walk with her, because Celia, at least, is her friend.

Thus she delivers her safely to the car and watches her go. She turns back, her mind a kaleidoscope of now and then, shards waiting to form a pattern, a meaning from the broken world. She imagines the world as a fallen place, its material blighted and evil, all goodness having left it to its own corruption. There is a bleakness inside her that is endless winter. This is the meaning of her mother's death. She can create no other reality from the evidence.

Lies, she tells herself. They were lies her mother told her. No magic. No Euterpe, no transformation. Her mother had told her she would be safe under the violin's protection, yet it was while she played that the violin was smashed.

Yes, her mother lied. She waits for a meaning to present itself to her other than this bitter truth.

None is forthcoming.

From the shadow a pair of eyes is watching her make her way through the snow. Now, a figure steps out from the doorway where it studied her. She meets those eyes, feeling their dark intensity boring into her – an expression that only a few days ago would have raised aggression in her body. Now she shrugs.

What does she care that Riley is here? She stops and they exchange nods of recognition.

"How you doing?" he asks, those dark eyes vacant, a kind of deadness in them, a fatalism that has swept over him. A single objective now driving him, with no other thought:

Her.

Wonder surfaces in Donitza from deep down. A connection she never expected to make, it surprises her and once more gives her the fleeting ghost of hope. She resigns herself to him with an exhalation, and he walks beside her, down the road to the house. At the door, she says:

"Did you leave something for me, earlier today?"

A fleeting self-deception settles in her, in the way that thirsting travellers imagine oases in the desert. She reasons: *Perhaps the world is not entirely broken if selflessness grows in unexpected places.*

To her pleasure, he nods. He shoots her a smile, almost boyish. She responds with a flicker at the corner of the mouth. She needs this, she realises. A man who is interested in her physical presence.

A scenario floats in front of her – perhaps his muscular, long body will warm the cold inside her, numb the pain for a moment.

"Why don't you come in," she commands after a second's thought.

Further down the road, in the gripping ache of the night, she hears a fox bark.

Cold. So cold, she thinks. *Poor thing.*

But she cannot tell if it is anguish or laughter that echoes around her.

*

The night air is freezing around the child lost in the woods, seeping into her bones stroking them with a drowsing ache as if crystals are forming in her joints. Her teeth are chattering and the strength in her limbs is being steadily devoured by cold. Time is an illusion. There is only one moment to which her attention is nailed, which repeats over and over in her mind. An indelible image. Her mother, dropping from the mountainside, her eyes still seeking her daughter among the mass of moving figures. The film plays on a loop and starts again. Beside the sound track the film carries a track for the emotions – wretched helplessness and incomprehension, over and over.

She feels she may be dying and instinctively looks skyward as if an answer might be written there. Above her, through the pine trees, the great glowing stars are winter white, not yellow as they often are, shining with a glittering intensity, twinkling because semi-visible creatures are swarming between her and them in the otherspace her mother spoke of sometimes. Her mother is there, too, making the starlight dance.

The cold in her body shuts off. A warm lethargy takes hold of her, and spreads through her limbs, as if they are lead, or stone. *This is death*, she realises, and shrugs helplessly, considering herself in the abstract, a small thing of flesh soon to return to earth. She feels no pain. Only sadness. *Such a short life,* she thinks, as if she had heard about herself somewhere.

Her eyes begin to dim. She sits on the hard ground huddled against a tree trunk and waits.

She looks up through the encroaching darkness and sees something whose presence she does not understand.

A figure is moving toward her through the woods. A female form, proceeding slowly with gentle movements as if she is made of shadow or subtleness, so that only those with the eyes to look can see her. The figure is wearing a red and yellow peasant dress covered with a shawl, and there is a comb in her hair. Donitza sees her and she sees Donitza in a moment of mutual acknowledgement. The figure smiles down on the little girl who is a ragged bundle of despair. She points toward her a pipe – a musical instrument she lifts in her hand and twirls between her fingers.

There is a silence that bridges, like the communication from a painting on a wall to the viewer. New understanding fills the young girl's mind and following an instinct Donitza begins to sing a song her mother taught her. It is the song her mother sang when gathering moonbeams in jars. She sees her in half-hallucination, overlaid on the woman with the pipe who stands before her. A line of glass cylinders standing by the wall, washed at night with white lunar light from a pregnant moon. Her mother would only finish the song after she covered the jars with a cork stopper and dripped wax around the rim to seal them. Then she would hide them away.

Two weeks later, when the moon was dark, her mother would pull them out and stand them in a circle on the table, the night black outside. Then she would sing the same song she had sung before.

What happened next was at first so gentle it felt like it could be pure imagination. Almost imperceptibly the jars would respond by emitting a subtle light. Then, as the song went on, the light grew brighter, until the whole room was bathed in moonglow that cast dark shadows at the room's edge.

As she sat with her daughter in the milkwhite light, her mother said:

"Learn this song. It is a song of conservation. Sing it now with me."

Donitza can feel her mouth moving as her mother bid. Her body floods with new vitality – weak and sickly at first, but growing more potent with each note. The vision of her mother fades and the silent woman standing in the snowbound woods reappears from the darkness. Donitza senses something – the warm tickle in the nose of herbs and spice, the summer flowers in a meadow, the richness of bread baked in clay. She sings more loudly.

The woman watches Donitza as the song grows, waits a while longer, then seemingly satisfied moves on, disappearing into the wood as if she is the wood herself. Donitza sees her transform into a shambling creature of leaves and branches that eventually blow away, as if the forest is reabsorbing a being that is part of itself.

When she is gone, Donitza closes her eyes and continues to sing up her strength.

When she opens them again, her mind now more alert, she can sense every pine needle around her, the movement of every creature. She exhales and senses another life nearby that has come to watch her. A fox is sitting by her, moonlight striking its head and making its features stand out like a drawing in ink.

It rises and pads in close, its red fur noticeably red even in the starlight and it barks a long high bark that cracks her further from the cold's hard grip. It comes closer, breathing into her face, scrabbling around her, nudging, licking her hands and face until she wakes fully from the hypothermic dream she was wandering in, urgently aware of a deep need for warmth.

"A fire," she says. "I need fire."

The fox tugs her sleeve insistently. She doesn't know if she is dreaming or already dead, but she pulls herself to her feet, still clutching the violin case that bangs against her knees and she stands swaying, a creature of the elements registering semi-consciously the darkness of the forest. The outline of the fox is ahead of her. It looks back with lambent eyes.

She steps toward it. It moves away from her now, swiftly leading her through the forest that stands expectantly silent, like the moment when someone speaks a truth better left unsaid. It follows a track, forwards and onwards. Exhausted, she follows, not knowing where else to go. She stumbles through iron pine uprights, the crisp snow beneath her feet unfelt because the cold has reached inside of her. The song is wearing out, the moonbeams nearly burned, she realises. She cannot go on much longer, the fatigue is winding out around her, a hundred thousand spiders weaving a web against which she cannot struggle, the air a resistant net in which she is trapped.

Cold. Dying. Dying. She thinks the words and knows they are true. Her breaths are more spectral than before as if the air she breathes out has less soul. In the distance she hears the voice of a man and smells on a waft of air the pungent urgency of cooked meat. A stew. Lights ahead. She walks on in a dream, the fox slinking ahead of her, its head low, looking from left to right as if hunting. *A fire. Warmth.* A final effort.

She is stumbling toward an encampment. A group of men in the distance. She will ask them for food.

She sees the Captain outlined in the light and a shock of despair and anger pulses through her. She eyes his face from the shadows. The fox looks to her, and is gone.

A hand closes over her mouth and powerful arms lift her.

*

In Celia's living room all is ordered as it has been for decades.

"You must be cold. Do you want a cup of tea?" Donitza asks in mimicry of the English, and considers the English meaning of English tea. It is something she has learned from Celia, this business of tea with milk. It has a different effect from coffee, she reflects, refreshing in a more subtle way. *To think: putting milk in tea!* The idea had disgusted her once.

Riley pulls a half bottle from his pocket. Bell's whisky.

"How about something more warming?" he says. "Got any ice?"

She looks at him ironically and tells him she won't be long.

In the kitchen she opens the door to the winter night. Reaching up she breaks off a thick icicle pending from the gutter and brings it back in to crack into shards in a bowl. She lifts the bowl and takes two glasses with her to the room where he is waiting, a dark silent entity.

"Will these do?"

He smiles at her, breathing the scent of her body. She does not mind him, he calculates. This break has made her more pliable. But he's never one to leave a thing to chance.

"Perfect." He pours the amber spirit into two glasses and says. "Got any water? It's better with a bit of water."

She turns again, goes to the kitchen and fills a jug. When she comes back he is sitting back looking at her with narrowed eyes, drawn in on himself. He lifts the jug and drops a splash of water in each glass.

"Drink," he says, nodding to her tumbler. "It'll do you good."

She traps her hair against the side of her neck, her head turned sideways, inhaling the foreign smell that stings the nostrils, before setting the drink to her lips and drawing some down. She likes it and nurses the glass in her hand rather than setting it down again.

"I want to –" She pauses for a moment to think what to say next. "I wanted to thank you. For the violin." She doesn't want to tell him it is a child's practice instrument nowhere near good enough for the use she wants to put it to, liable to lose its tuning and with a bad action difficult to play. "It was kind of you."

Riley coughs into his glass at that word again. *Kind.* He loves it that people see things for what they seem to be, not for what they are. *Most people are idiots*, he thinks, with some satisfaction that his view of the world has been reinforced again. *Except me.*

He plays the game back. "It was nothing," he says with a wave of the hand. "I saw how upset you were last night and I thought you needed something. Some support. You always seem so alone."

She takes another deep mouthful from the glass and doesn't know whether to laugh or cry. Was she so wrong about this man, then? Is it that her instinct that told her to avoid him at all costs was playing a trick on her? She sees Riley as an innocent boy unknowingly walking into one of the enclaves in her homeland seeded with anti-personnel mines, where children retrieving stray balls lose hands and feet in a moment of self-forgetfulness. She is the minefield, not him, it seems.

Her instinct was wrong.

So wrong, she thinks and while she looks up again with blurred vision to see him smiling there, reconsidering his soft pink lips and his black beard, she feels a tonal shift in the room.

It is difficult to identify at first. There are the blue and white porcelain figurines Celia dusts every day, and a stack of old LPs with Kenny Rogers at its top. There is the collection of white porcelain thimbles with the crests of the English towns and cities Celia has visited in her long life. All are now tinged with red. Her field of vision is swaying and she perceives the musician Riley as a creature in a woodland, salivating as he looks at her. He is not holding a drink any more, but a pipe with which he plays an elusively sweet tune. Now he stands on goat's legs and moves toward her and she struggles to move. In the crotch of this stinking goat is a tumescent penis garishly red. She feels sick and glares at her drink and then at him accusatorily.

The creature in front of her sways with delight at its own power and stumbles under the weight of its intention. She is amazed by it, this creature of nature, dark and violent. Riley comes closer and takes hold of her face, kissing her roughly. She is too disoriented to resist.

Her vision turns redder still. A crimson flow that paints him the colour of blood. Something wrong. Something very wrong. She tries to stand and walk away but her legs don't respond. She looks up at him as he starts to roughly unbutton her blouse, seeing him now for what he is.

"Do you believe in the Devil?" she asks, the question coming from nowhere, as he straightens his back and rips open her blouse with a violent movement.

She begins to struggle, her arms rising ineffectually to push him away and she shouts with helpless rage. He clamps his hand over her mouth and pulls her tight against his hard body. She bites his hand, turns her head and shouts a hoarse, angry shout. His eyes are black pits – a fall through desperation to nothingness, a dark emptiness into whose orbit she has strayed. She struggles again frantically, but she is weak and disoriented and she cannot stop his hand as he strikes her across her face, knocking her, with an explosion of white light into unconsciousness.

*

In the wood the stranger holding his hand over the child's mouth swings her into the air then lopes away, quivering branches dislodging snowfall in flurries. There is a shout behind her. A sentry has noted their presence. The man lopes on. She struggles in his arms, but he presses her tighter. There is a harsh burst of fire, flashes of white light and the trees shake around her. More shouting. She begins to notice a tension in the man as he holds her in front of him – a trembling fight as he pushes forward almost desperate. Now panting, the man lopes on. She can hear his breath in starts and gasps, coarse in the air. There is more shouting in the distance. Guns blaze behind her. The man lopes on.

Snow begins to fall heavily around her, drifting down in lazy flight. Still the man lopes on.

An immeasurable interval. Fear in the night. The brush of firs against her face, the smell of the pine sap and the must of the under-canopy. The shouting dies away behind her. She can feel him trembling as he carries her, his breath turning to gasps. Moments in which he mutters to himself.

He comes to a stop, standing stock still, his hand clamped over her mouth. She looks up to see his head silhouetted against the starlit sky, cocked to one side, listening. He waits. Waits a while longer. The forest watches in silence.

He ducks, pushes in through a brake of ferns and turns with concentrated attention to rearrange them. There is no snow here, the canopy above and the line of a scarp has prevented the snowfall gathering to leave a telltale spoor. She sees him vaguely, this figure in camouflage. A soldier. There is a tear to his jacket and around it a dark stain that has spread out in the night like dye in a pond.

Satisfied that the ferns are right, he stops and listens for a moment longer until he is sure the men who were following have gone. He draws back with her toward the scarp, and she sees in the silver light a crack in a rock face, a narrow opening through which he gestures her to go. She walks in, head bowed. He follows, sits at the entrance and motions her to lie down. There is a bed here and a sleeping bag she climbs into, weak with weary cold. She smells the animal smell of the man – he has been here for weeks, she realises in a flash of lucidity. Sweat and the smell of dirt and something rotting. He pours a liquid from a flask and hands her a plastic cup, sweet and meaty. He gestures her to drink. Its warmth reaches down through her body like an embrace.

He sits in the opening, more a presence than a person as she lies awake, afraid to talk, afraid of everything, her body a long unending ache of misery. When she realises that she is too tired to cry then she finally tumbles off the edge of wakefulness into sleep.

She has escaped at last from a day that will never leave her.

*

Memory.

Riley has memories, too.

Hot angry nights rise before his eyes. How his mother would dress him down for his teen clumsiness.

"Don't clatter around like that," she would tell the insomniac boy keen to step out at any hour.

In the sullen interior of his thoughts he would say: "A gigantic fucking house, and she has to hear me every fucking time."

What could he do? A teenager who couldn't sleep with the night all around him. It stretched on forever: out over the island city, out past the twinkling lights of the other island across the strait, out across the black expanse of the sea that lapped at the shore, a muscular giant moving beneath its surface. The night went on forever: in one direction ferries ploughed through it, in another it rose and climbed like a raven beyond the white bluff of chalk cliff, where the MoD had planted a warship's masts on a hill, flying out past the empty fields beyond to housing estates and woods, casting shadow over all.

He sometimes wondered if it was the drugs he took that made him like this. Enough dope to tranq an ox. Enough speed to keep him dancing all night. Whizzing like a maniac. Sometimes his ineffectual mother seeing his wired frame, his white darting eyes, put it down to *hormones*.

The missing element in the picture was Riley's father. Six years before he had jumped in a sports car with a blonde in her 20s. He threw his past over his shoulder for a life in a former British colony. He had been salting his money away to the Seychelles for over a year before he left.

With the businessman's precision, he had made a calculation and handed over the house and a small fund with which his mother would never be uncomfortable, and by which her pension would be secured. Then he had vanished like a pantomime devil in a puff of smoke, the hellmouth opening not beneath him, but beneath Riley's mother. She had gone into mourning in a house big enough to pull up the drawbridge and lose contact with her friends.

When Riley couldn't sleep, sometimes he would lie staring at the sky with the windows thrown open to the sound of the sea steadily brushing along the shore. His sleep patterns didn't follow circadian rhythms reset by daylight. "I'm always an hour out, my sleep moves onwards, overlapping the day". Sometimes he blinked awake and asleep at the same time of the day but a few weeks later was a vampire waking in the night. "I have tides," he told himself with the teenager's self-rationalisation.

He would think of his dad in the dead times of night and imagine a letter or an email. A card, even.

None came.

At school, Riley wasn't liked. Something in his manner, like the old boy at the lake had said, made his schoolmates hate him. Class hatred? Maybe. Had it been the same at the Grammar School before the straitened reality of his father's departure? He wasn't sure. His mother could have sold up for his future, but instead clutched the house tight for her past, as if somehow her ex-husband might walk back in one day with a "sorry, Love. The traffic."

The only answer to the question of his disappearance was that his Dad hated him. He'd learned to embrace hatred after a while and hate back, so that hate became a part of him. He was bigger than the boys at the State school, and he could hurt them more because he hated them more. The world was all hate, really. Whether giving or receiving, hatred was its rule. Him, his father, his mother: a hate triangle the geometry of his life.

When he was a younger boy he had loved. He had loved the beach, for a start, spending days winding out the tides and winding them back in again under a baking sun.

Later, he sought solace there again. Finding the cold obduracy of the stones comforting, he would throw them with delight at the gulls, occasionally hitting one, but to his disappointment never killing it. When he got older and was alone, he developed the habit of smashing things when he could. He didn't know why, except it made him feel like he was in charge, that he controlled the fate of something. He had a thing about telephone boxes, laughing at how easy it was to smash a handset with just the right whipping action. A predictable outcome was easier to elicit destructively.

The night called to him. It always called, so that when the full moon settled over the water in the hot summer months he would feel exaltation in its white light and bathe in its presence. It was a release. On the beach late at night fishermen grew along its edge in clumps – all-nighters with lights on their hats who would hear the scrunch of stone behind them and turn to dazzle him if he walked too near.

Other parts of the beach were quiet. Sometimes he would walk from the tired old pier toward the eastern point and its inlet to a wide expanse of natural harbour. Sitting by a yacht's tender padlocked to a pillar he would watch the muscular water flexing as the current came in and out, drinking Vodka stolen from a shop, or Thunderbird, or anything. He never saw anyone down there. It suited him.

All these thoughts come to him now as he stands in the hallway of Celia's house. They come to him each day at some point, a habit that has become part of the grain of his consciousness, but tonight they feel more real. He pushes against them in his mind as he pulls open the door. He looks down at the snow outside, then back over his shoulder with fond pleasure at the scene he is about to leave.

Behind him in the living room, she is lying on the chair, a welt over her eye, staring with no emotion on her face, withdrawn into herself. He notices a sinking feeling in his stomach and acknowledges it. He doesn't care about the future any more, he realises. The control he seeks can only be created for a fleeting instant like a radioactive particle that decays on formation. Now he has had his moment of victory – forced her down – he wants the next stage of attention this act will bring him.

For now, a post-coital half-life has decayed and he feels empty. He closes the front door behind him, gently. There is no future.

The police will come, he tells himself with relief.

Walking up the road, he is distracted briefly by an illusion. A creature's prints impressed in the snow, maybe a small dog or a cat. He looks at them with distracted interest as he follows the same route.

With a trick in the way the snow has melted, the prints change in their regular rhythm. The close double prints of front foot and back foot in tracked pairs marking out the quadruple common time of 4/4 shift in their signature so that farther up the road they mark duple time. Unbidden in his mind's eye he sees a creature straightening upright to walk on its hind legs, polkaing through the snow in 2/4. For a few bars, the feet widen. The snow has melted where it lies over a hot outlet pipe buried beneath the pavement, leaving the print of a wider mark, each with a point, with a small segment of snow cleaving the apex. Finally, as they follow the path to the intersection with the busier road the prints overlap with those of human boots and shoes.

It is a bizarre effect which even Riley laughs at, though he shudders suddenly, as if the cold has struck into him.

*

When Celia arrives home, she finds Donitza lying on the sofa in the front room. The white and blue lady in glazed crinoline is on the mantelpiece and the set of thimbles is in the case on the wall just as it has always been. But Donitza is not right, Celia can see it straight away. She has pulled a jumper over her torn shirt and sits huddled, staring blank-eyed at the room. There is an angry mark around her eye.

With an instinct, Celia comes to her and puts her hand on her arm. A sudden insight.

"Who did this?" she asks. "Who?"

Donitza does not answer, staring blankly at the wall ahead; only an echoing silence and a brutal numbness fill her body. The walls are moving in and out in time with her breath and she has the tingling feeling of electricity in her palms and sickness in her stomach. Still she says nothing and so Celia, with an instinct that says "tread carefully", talks to fill the air.

"This town," she says with considered airiness. "It's almost genteel in places now compared to what it was – and that's not saying much. But it wasn't always this way, Dearie."

Donitza looks to her silently as Celia goes on. Celia is considering her experiences with a quiet thoughtfulness – reliving moments of walking through bombed-out streets, flaming tongues of buddleia and blood-red poppies sprouting from cleared sites where the Luftwaffe dropped death. She re-experiences the smell of coal smoke in the air, the quiet electric whine of trolley-buses and copies of *The Picture Post* and *Everybody* and *Woman's Own* in the newsagent window. The city back then...

"In the fifties you saw a uniform on every street and a pub on every corner. In those days there were no traffic schemes and bypasses, just a straight walk from the dockyard to the city centre." She circles around the subject. She speaks of Ruby's – The *Standard* pub – where the tally bands off sailors' caps from a fleet that had once dominated the world found a haven to be pinned. She remembers some of the girls who worked the surrounding streets. Her friend, a Sunday School teacher, once said of that road from the dockyard, *A creeping level of moral decline in a straight line from Ruby's to the dockyard gate.* Carefully. Steady as she goes.

"Back then, girls got into trouble. Sometimes a sailor or a soldier or a dockyard worker forced a girl to give him what he wanted, when he was broke, or drunk. Sometimes he didn't even know he'd forced her."

She pauses a moment, looking into the depths behind Donitza's emotionless face.

"Come here," the old woman says, and gently balances on the arm of the sofa, tilting the younger woman's head toward her and resting its crown in the crook of her neck.

She is expecting Donitza to cry. But there are no tears. Just the hard look of anger that she saw in some of those girls back then. She helped when she was younger. A volunteer for the church.

She remembers those girls. This city, a transit point for tens of thousands of sailors, soldiers and other transients, a place with a tradition of toughness and brutality. A frontier town. *Is it different, now? So much?*

Rape was an exotic noun they hardly ever used back then. It was not used when she was a young woman. They saved it for later generations.

She puts her hand out and wipes Donitza's cheek with the back of her hand, gently touching old fingers to young skin.

"After all these years, I remember. It isn't your fault." Celia pulls away to look at Donitza earnestly, troubled by her lack of response. "You must tell someone. You will, won't you?"

Under the urgency in those eyes Donitza tips her head forward.

Immediately, Celia goes to the hall and reaches for the telephone.

*

The police arrive in 20 minutes. Celia lets into the house a thickset woman Sergeant with brown curly hair poking from beneath her hat, followed by a gaunt young CPSO, with a watery gaze, continually blinking as he adjusts to his newly purchased contact lenses.

After they knock the snow off their shoes during a low conversation with Celia in the corridor, they enter the living room and the Sergeant measures Donitza with her experienced eye.

She is ready to talk, the Sergeant thinks, and takes on the empathetic body language that is so often effective: head lowered, leaning forward, forehead creased. She tells her gently: "Hello, are you all right? I understand you want to report an assault?"

Donitza looks at the uniform and an emotion comes to her, growling like a watchdog, closing a part of her mind. *Shame. Anger. Helplessness.* These are the intruders this watchdog will not let pass.

The young musician does not look at the Sergeant, but stands and walks. She will not accept sympathy. No sympathy at all. That is the enemy. That is weakness.

The Sergeant leans back and looks to Celia.

"She said she would talk to someone," the old woman explains.

It is not the first time the Sergeant has seen this. They try different approaches over the next half hour, but Donitza won't open her mouth. Not a word. She glares defiance, denies approach.

After a while the Sergeant speaks again to Celia. "I'm sorry. There is nothing we can do if she won't speak to us. Perhaps you can have a word?"

*

In the icy cave, the newly-made orphan makes a decision.

She will not talk to this soldier. She does not know who he is, and she will not speak with him. She has decided this.

He is sitting in the entrance, and he, too, does not speak. She can see his silhouette, unmoving in the morning light as the brightness intensifies. A cold air breathes into the dark space from the forest on the far side of where he is seated.

She waits like this, watching him for what feels like hours, and with growing uncertainty realises he has not moved at all. She climbs out of the sleeping bag and creeps toward him. He still does not move. She stands over him and sees that the blood on his shoulder has congealed to a red-black stain. She also notices an older, deep cut on his hand, where a black swelling has started to bloat the fingers.

When she touches him with a timid finger, he does not move until she is pushing him so hard he begins to tip over. He starts with a brief grunt, after which he falls on his side.

She stares at him, paralysed for a moment, wondering what he is doing. Playing a trick on her? A game. She looks more closely and hesitantly reaches her hand to his neck, feeling for the telltale beat her mother taught her – the tempo of life. The rhythm is faint and erratic, coming in triplet beats with large pauses between. She looks at his hand again and sniffs analytically. A medley of smells. The chemicals of a gun, the woodland, dirt, and underneath it all as a counterpoint, a sweet smell. *Poisoned.* He is dying from the poison his own body is making, she realises with a mind that leaps to life.

She remembers her mother's voice, talking of how a dark spirit will force the body to eat itself if left unchecked. The spirit must be driven out by the power of heat and astringent herbs.

She feels the skin on his brow and then on his neck again to double confirm the diagnosis. In the cold light he is as cold as the day. She decides that here is something she can set right. She lights a fire in the entrance, gathering pine cones to spark to life and small pieces of kindling from around the doorway, dry as bone and brittle as glass.

His sightless eyes are staring into a world she cannot see, and she wonders if this is the manifestation of the Ecstasy her mother once told her about.

"The Ecstasy," she thinks of her mother talking to her in earnest. They are in the cottage, with the shutters closed over the windows. Outside, the night is darkening, the forest a hush of held breath, its eyes directed toward the low building. She imagines all creatures of the forest there, listening to her mother's wisdom.

"The Ecstasy is the moment at which the veil between the worlds is lifted. The questions the querent asks at such times are answered with words that are bigger questions. The lifting of the veil means the querent sees the immense connections beyond the surfaces of our world."

Her mother pauses a moment. She has finished laying out a circle of thirteen candles on the tabletop and she takes the moment to look at her daughter. "Unless you speak in the original tongue of the Universe, you have only Earthly words as signifiers – thus life can be spoken of only partially because the bond between word and world is too distant."

Her daughter watches her mother light the candles in steady intervals with a spill lit from a lantern, singing a low song as she goes, and between this broken melody, explaining: "Some people believe that those who speak like this have their senses clouded. But that is wrong. Very wrong. It is *our* senses that are clouded. We see the world through the glass darkly while those who speak in the original tongue see clearly, and are misunderstood for it."

She finishes lighting the thirteenth candle with the long wooden spill that has now nearly burned down. "Men have said it this way in the past and they were right, but even the words *they* used were inaccurate. Why? Because they did not use the language of the universe, lost when the forces that made the matter of the world abandoned it." She shrugs. "This is the meaning of the word *ineffable*."

Her mother tells her that she is going to open a channel to the other world this night, and that her daughter is to listen and remember anything that seems important to her. She will ask her about it later.

"Remember what I say," she says. "Because I will not."

Then her mother takes a flask from the corner of the room, where it has been left to stand in daylight and moonlight for 40 days and nights. She pours from it a viscous liquid that smells bitter and pungent, and drinks it down after reciting an incantation.

She resumes the incantation, staring upwards at the ceiling once she has shuddered the liquid down her neck.

After ten minutes, her irises constrict to the tiniest points. She shakes, moving her head from side to side in a rhythmic sway. Now the irises distend until her hazel eyes are great black holes reflecting the candle's soft yellow light. Looking closely, Donitza thinks that when she is staring into her mother's eyes, she is staring into heaven.

The noises her mother makes over the next two hours as she lies and twitches in the darkness after the candles have burned down and spread their wax corpses across the table in formless puddles are inarticulate sounds. A while longer her mother frets and cries and whimpers. No words come.

A while after this, Donitza sees that her mother has fallen asleep, and not knowing what else to do, she covers her in a blanket and goes to bed.

The next morning her mother looks at her with still-cosmic eyes and asks her what she heard. When Donitza reports on the evening's events, her mother goes quiet, searching inside herself and feeling the profundity of the previous night, the emotional truth of the moment. How can she tell her daughter in words that will make sense? She shrugs and after thinking about it for a while, says resignedly: "Hah. Sometimes the magic works, sometimes not. Some things cannot be said. That is the meaning of ineffable, after all."

She never repeats the experiment. But afterwards, she says for the first time: "Bad men are coming," as if she has seen something she should not.

Donitza realises the soldier is in the Ecstasy, lying there on the iron ground with a radio next to him. The radio is dead, with a bullet hole in it.

From time to time he calls out *in sotto voce* using a language she does not know that could either be the ineffable language or the language of man. She wonders if these really can be the words of the first language until she hears English words she understands. *United Nations* is one such word. Another is *peacekeeper*, which for some reason she has picked up from a traveller passing the door. At other times he speaks in her mother's language and shouts out: "I can't stop them," and "Call it in now, urgent, urgent." Then he turns his head to her and looks her in the eyes, and says with a fevered intensity:

"Do you believe in the devil?"

He sits up, his eyes figuring something in the distance. She notices the bristles on his chin are auburn in the light. He reaches out his hand.

"He's there. Watching us!"

She turns her head, to see a fox's brush disappearing into the ferns. The soldier falls back.

Donitza no longer fears the soldier. He believes in the Red Man, she supposes, like the man who brought the trouble to her and her mother. But she does not fear him, nor his Red Man. Instead, when she looks at the soldier with his auburn stubble she sees only a patient wracked with poisons. *She must save him.*

Stepping past him at the cave entrance, she heads into the snow. There will be no fall tonight. A full moon is due, and she must act quickly. In haste she recalls the formulary her mother has embedded in her mind. The plants with virtues to slow the blood and the virtues to take heat. The power of the herb to dilute poison in the veins, and the seed to break the cycle of death. She remembers the influences of the planets they are under and the houses where they live. She spends the day circling, grubbing under rocks to find the roots of plants whose souls have gone to sleep beneath the snowblanket, all the while one ear cocked for the tread of soldiers.

She is shivering when she returns, as the short winter day turns to evening. In the distance she can hear wolves calling to each other, and the sound of a chopper's blades slicing the air into chunks of noise.

The fire has burned down and the soldier is unconscious, his exhalation a ghost itself, so that she wonders if the living part of him is about to leave, just like the forces that created the universe departed, leaving it to roll on indifferently through time.

We are abandoned, she thinks, realising with growing dread that he is now her only connection. *We live in an abandoned world. There is no one to save us.*

She looks toward him, but cannot see him through her tears.

Part 3

WHEN Celia opens the door after the bell's ring has thinned to silence, a single thought shoots through her mind with shocking clarity, as the cold daylight reaches round the exposed jamb into her hallway. *His eyes are so green.*

The stranger is standing in the snow, panting against the cold, blowing on his delicate white fingers. In the half second in which her imagination takes flight, a breathghost materialises before her, seemingly presenting the profile of a face in anguish. Shaken, she turns her head sideways, reaches the flat of her hand to her temple and taps it, as if to knock out soot. She looks forward again. The apparition has gone.

The stranger has a narrow face beneath a russet fur hat, and a similarly coloured neatly cropped goatee beard that protrudes to a point. When she first opens the door, he is running his pointed tongue around his lips in a slow circle. His green eyes narrow as they focus on her, as if she is a puzzle to be worked out. His smile reveals sharp white teeth like those of a baby, small in the mouth. She shudders against the ice-bearing wind.

"Hello, I called by yesterday," he says in a voice with slight softenings and slowings in the syllables – the "t" and "d" consonants pronounced with delicacy, the sound nearly unprojected as the tongue touches the palate only gently. He snuffles against the cold, his head turning as he draws winter air through his nostrils.

She blinks at his words and sends a filing clerk back through the recesses of her memory. Did he call by yesterday? In the increasing scatter of her life she is not sure, but she has a feeling he did not. He points to a narrow shelf in the hall, next to the place where visitors hang their coats, and reaches in.

"Here," he says, lifting a card from it.

She wonders why she didn't notice it there before. The filing clerk returns, looking embarrassed, empty hands palm upwards, after the scurry through the disordered files of her mind. He deals her the card and she fleetingly wonders if somehow he manifested it from thin air.

"Can I come in?" he says, dispelling the suspicion with such an appealing smile, despite his strange appearance, that she melts.

"Yes, yes," she answers, and shows him through to the cramped living room.

Something in him of Charlie, she thinks, remembering a day on a beach in the summer of her youth. Ice-creams and the penny arcades at Brighton. A day out. Donkey riding. The slow bored gait and the musk of four-legged slavery near the rearing bulk of the pier. Beneath its shadow, illicit kisses, surreptitiously stolen, redolent with the sugared smell of rock. All this dominoed by his smile. She follows him in, reading his card as he sits.

Reynold Lissitch
Counsellor

By the time she has read it he is leaning forward and turning the knob on the gas fire, the one she always struggles to light with its built-in sparker. He turns it with a deft twist and the gas jumps to life immediately, sending a blue spectre into the room that turns to nothing in a half second, but leaves the impression of a creature, dog-like, low, with a pointed snout.

"You don't mind," he asks without asking. He darts his green eyes at her. They take on the fireglow from the gas mantle. "Please, sit," he says waving an expansive hand.

"Thank you," Celia says, still bewildered. "But I don't need a counsellor. I don't know anything about this..."

"You don't?" he says, an expression of disappointment fleeting across his face. "But how do you say this? Ah. We have our wires crossed. Yes, you know we do."

"We do?"

"We do. – Yes?" he waits a moment as the command goes in. "I am not here for you. Of course, no. But you know this. You joke with me, yes!"

He slaps his thin hands on his lap and laughs, turning his face to the ceiling and drawing back his lips in a wide, white-toothed smile, sniffing the air like a wild animal.

"Your guest. She is not well. That is why I am here. As we discussed. Before."

And so he talks, impressing on her in the clearest terms how vital it is he sees the musician upstairs. He is here to help her. The police. He mentions the police and more urgency and the fact that her evidence is vital. And so on. He is all heat and animation, and she feels herself picking up his heat herself. She glows in his presence, as he speaks with deftness and craft and clarity and obfuscation.

"A lovely house, you have lived here a long time alone and now you have a friend. We must help her, that is why I am here to see her get better, thanks to you."

And all the while, he gestures and smiles and nods, and she finds that she smiles and nods back. Thus his speech works on her confused mind so that eventually she agrees that, yes, she will talk to Donitza and let her know he is here to see her, as they agreed yesterday evening after the police left.

Upstairs, Donitza is lying beneath her covers when she hears doorbell's ring announcing an arrival. *Who is it now? Him again? Him?*

Since the previous night, after three painfully hot baths which took away for a while the feeling of dirt in her body, she has been in a holding pattern. The way an aircraft flies 8s over an airport, waiting to land. That is how she has been. Cycling over and over again, withdrawn into herself. Events have piled up now, stacked one on the other – her life, the last few days of the unending disaster. Her mother's legacy is a jumble of useless knowledge, misleading information and fantasy. She realises at last that her mother gave her nothing.

This thought brings her to a decision and she climbs out of bed, gathering her few belongings into her camouflage rucksack.

She thinks of how her mother died, and tries to piece the death together into a shape that makes sense. There is no gestalt. No defining moment that will draw everything together. She thinks of the Christians who lived below her in the valley when she was a girl and their neighbours the Muslims. How they at least had certainties, however nonsensical. A God and an Adversary. It was never like that for her when she was a girl. Always her mother danced on the edge of the world, a flame on the side of a branch, sparking here, wandering there. Always alive, but never fixed – unlike the candles she saw through the windows of churches.

Her mother was ever-shifting, unpredictable; the maverick ship of her beliefs, never steered by a fixed star, wandered with the comets. The same has happened with her daughter, both emotionally and physically.

"This is what you get if you base your life on an empty promise: a rootless life," she thinks as she tightens the buckle on her rucksack in preparation to run away again, as if escape were a destination.

Celia appears at the door, a hesitant smile. She registers the paleness of the girl and her heart reaches out to her, an intent that rushes from her body toward the girl and envelops her in kindness and care if only the girl would notice.

"Janey," she says, her eyes unfocussed a moment before she corrects herself and hands her the card from Lissitch. "Donitza. There is someone downstairs who wants to see you."

Donitza weighs Celia's presence. *So much sadness she has never expressed.* The musician sits on the bed and speaks with a deliberate slowness, as if unsure how her own voice works as she asks the question that has troubled her. *A distraction*, she thinks. Something to pull her out of herself for a moment. She places the card Celia offers her on the bed and looks at the old woman, pale in the winter light.

"Tell me about Janey," she says. "You never said what happened to her."

Celia slumps next to her on the bed, a dead weight overburdened by the mass of her own aged body. This is grief, she supposes. The weight of grief which she has carried and which has not, as she was told it would, trickled away over time – the memories leaving a trail behind her, gold dust from a ruptured bag, blowing away at last. But these memories have maintained their mass. Obstinately, they have not decreased or faded. Perhaps they have grown heavier over the years. And why? Because there is no release.

Celia's eyes cloud over.

"Janey was a beautiful girl," she says, adding with a wistful voice. "I don't know. Maybe she still is." She lets out a sigh. "My daughter's daughter."

She remembers the night she first came to her. News that her own pregnant daughter in the throes of labour and her husband had been killed in a car crash rushing to hospital. The horror of that moment counterbalanced by her. A little miracle. Plucked from the scene of death.

"I lost my daughter, but here, here was a compensation, and I promised the memory of my girl that I would look after her. Oh, she was a whirl of sunshine. A smile in the afternoon and laughter in the morning. I could measure the days with her laughter. From the moment she came to us, me and Charlie – her granddad – we loved her so much. 'Golden Chuckles' he called her. *The sunshine girl.*"

Donitza sits back on the bed, detaching herself from Celia to hear her objectively, making a picture of this other childhood – an alternative to her own.

"She was a delight every day. Running back from school, playing with her friends. Whatever she did, people loved her. She grew up from a little smiler into a tall, pretty girl that just made people's lives brighter. I mean that too, mind," she adds with sudden clarity in her eyes. "Everyone loved her. That's why her leaving was such a shock. It didn't make any sense then, and it still doesn't. She just walked out of our lives."

"What? What do you mean?"

"What I say. One evening she went out for a walk. No-one saw where to. It was late and she shouted over her shoulder with a carefree song in her voice: 'I'm off out, Mum.' – She called me Mum. 'Where you going, so late?' I asked. She never replied, not properly. 'Just out, Mum!' What business was it of mine? She was a young woman. And that was the last time I saw her, last time I heard her voice."

She wrings her hands, pulling at the port-wine-stained skin near her knuckles with her crooked fingers as she works circular anguish on them. "I keep wondering if it was something I said. They found her clothes on the beach. Washed up at the Hot Walls. And nothing else of her. I wonder if she went for a swim and got lost in the water. But she went, and she never came back. And, oh my, I miss her so much!"

A single tear drips from her eyes and she pulls a folded tissue from her sleeve and blows her nose. *The years of loneliness. The waiting. The pain.* All accumulated here, now, in this contraction of sorrow into a dark star that sheds endless shadow on her life.

Celia shakes herself.

"Well, there it is. And then you come here, and you are so like her. And now you..." She stops a moment, a forceful clarity in her voice. "I don't want to see you hurt. There has been enough pain. I know what happened, last night, Janey. I knew the minute I came in. I don't know who, but I knew what. You've got to see someone. Tell someone. I said so last night. Please. For me."

Donitza comes back into herself. The distraction is gone and she feels the crushing weight of her own life, her own story sitting on her chest, a night goblin in a dream.

Celia's eyes fix on the camouflage rucksack. She sees how the bag is bulging with a giveaway tightness. She reaches over to it.

"You've packed this," she says in a voice half tinged with accusation. "Why have you packed it?" Celia asks, her eyes dull once more. "You can't go again. Listen, there's someone here to help you..."

Donitza can feel a growing tide of revulsion rising up. Like the sea, ready to pull her away again, take her on its currents and float her away, off this island. Always away to somewhere new.

"I can go where I like," she answers, with a cutting edge in her voice. "You're not my mother or my grandmother. I'm not your Janey. I'm not here to be owned and petted and to fill the hole in your life. I'm me. I'm my own person with my own life. Just leave me alone!" she shouts with real anger.

"But –"

"Go. *Leave me alone.* Leave me!"

She turns her back and hears Celia go.

She stands and looks out from her window at the snow-covered back gardens, the neat squares and the vestiges of hedges stuck beneath the great white oppressive blanket. *That's it.* Donitza's mind is made up. She will head out into the snow. She must get away from this place, from these people. She has done the thing she promised herself she would never do: get tangled and lost in the trackless woods of relationship and friendship and enmity. She was alone when she came here. There was pure clean whiteness all around her, not pain, not remembrance. *There are ferries, there are roads from here. These are the best things about this town – the ways out*, she thinks with metal bitterness sitting in the back of her mouth.

"Where will you go?" A man's voice asks as if it is from nowhere, or every point in the room.

Startled, she turns to see Lissitch standing in the doorway. His red hair and green eyes are so unearthly they draw from her an involuntary gasp. His hands are pushed into his coat pockets, a russet coat that shimmers with a sleek shine that is somehow alive, as if made of living hair, or fur. She blinks; the illusion goes. Just a coat. An ordinary coat.

"Who are you?"

He pulls a box of cigarettes from his pocket and taps it against his palm so one juts from the pack.

"Smoke?" he answers, proffering the box.

"I don't," she lies. "I never have."

A glimmer of amusement comes into his green eyes; a smile flickers across his face, animating it with a playfulness she finds beguiling, charming. He shrugs.

"You're right. I'm trying to give up, myself."

He flicks the cigarette back into its pack. As if from nowhere - another small packet from which he tips dark fleshy sweetness into his palm.

"You want one of these?" he smiles, shaking the packet of raisins.

She steps away from him warily, somehow getting tangled with the legs of the bed and falling on to it, all the while her eyes on him. She draws up her legs so that her chin is resting on her knees, her hands clutching her shins protectively and watches him move in a semi-circle around the bed. In the corner of the room is a small chair with some clothes on it. He lifts them carefully, puts them to one side and sits at it. He does not move for five breaths, looking down at the open case on the floor where the broken violin sits.

Eventually, he says: "You could get that fixed, you know."

He speaks nonchalantly, then turns his seagreen eyes to her. She feels a force in them, that takes her breath away. An intent, a purpose that she cannot quite understand but which both appeals to her and puts her on her guard.

She says: "Who are you?"

She feels afraid of him, this strange thin man with the narrow nose and goatee beard.

"I mean why not get it fixed?" he continues, as if to himself. "There are people who could do it. I play, too. So I know."

She looks at the crack, the broken join at the heel of the neck and shakes her head.

"That time has gone," she says, answering in this way perhaps because of the wariness he has woken in her. "I won't play again."

"You won't play again. You don't smoke. What am I to make of you?" he asks with a flat expression that gives nothing away. He waits a moment and continues. "But you know, I hear you are very good! Someone told me you play as if you've always played. Music is in your family? Perhaps that is down to your mother's influence..?"

She shoots him a fiery look, her head rising involuntary revealing a defiant, angry chin.

"What do you know about my mother?" she retorts.

He turns his head with little shakes, a tic he has, and sniffs the air again, quick snuffling movements. A short laugh catches in his throat.

"What do we know about our mothers, any of us? I know nothing of mine. Perhaps I never had one." He shrugs and glances at her again, a sideways look, appraising her. He goes on:

"But if your mother taught you, why would you stop now? You've brought this little confection of soundbox and gut and peg and bow all this way with you – Why stop for the sake of a knock? Such is not the way to go on in life, don't you agree?"

She remains silent, staring suspicion at him. He shakes another raisin from the packet and puts it in his mouth, chewing it thoughtfully with tiny, precise movements. He seems oblivious to her discomfort, and this in an odd way makes her discomfort go, as if she has made up the reasons for it herself.

"Can't you see it's broken?" she says, exasperated.

"Yes, yes, it is broken. For now. And you? Are you broken, too? Is this what you really tell me with *I won't play again?*"

"There is no reason to play," she says. "Only a lie."

"Many wonderful things have been fathered by a lie."

He chews a while longer, his head moving from side to side as if he is less interested by the flow of the conversation than in taking in more of the room and simply being in her presence, sitting there, defenceless, helpless in her coop. He licks his lips and swallows the fruit.

"Can I tell you a story?" he replies.

She shrugs.

"It is an old story," he goes on. "It is like this. – And stay with me, because the story has truths in it that many have forgotten. – At the very beginning of time, when the world was brand new and when God was still dusting off the lanterns he'd hung in the sky, when the stars were brighter in the heavens than they are today because the world sparkled with its own newness, there was a man called Adam. You may have heard of him. His name meant The Red Man, and he lived in the garden God had planted for him. One day, he looked around and he saw the animals moving in pairs, each coupled of their kind, and he asked God if he, too, could have a mate. God chuckled at his request and agreed.

"Just as he had made Adam from the red earth, God made his wife Lilith from the left-over fabric of the night sky. But with God there was always a catch – something that made his kindness troublesome. Lilith was filled with the wisdom of stardust. And with deep, unfathomable darkness, too.

"Adam was pleased with his woman, and commanded her to live with him. But Lilith, being made of the night sky, had the winds as her natural home, not the plodding red clay where Adam lived. As such, she criticised the way he lived, because she knew the ways of the world in a way he did not. She could see from high up the whole surface of Creation and understood some of the mechanism beneath. She chided Adam for his slow-wittedness. At night she hung stars in her hair and bewitched the creatures of the Garden so they came to her. They worshipped her. The kine, the swine and the serpent all alike. It was not long before Adam grew jealous and they quarrelled. That was the day he struck her. Lilith was angry with Adam, and she told him that if he did that again, she would turn the animals of the Garden against him.

"When Adam told God of his woes, God, who was a mischievous being, roared with laughter. He told Adam he would give him what he wanted: a wife who was like himself, made of his own bones, and he took a rib from Adam's body and fashioned another woman whom he called Eve.

"Lilith could see the humour in what God had done, for Adam thought that because she was of his flesh he could have dominion over her as he had control over his own fingers. This Eve knew that Adam was the stronger of the two, though God had made Eve intelligent and brave. One day, a rumour came to her from the Serpent that he had once struck Lilith, and this is why she kept her distance from them both. Eve was always one to listen to the sound advice of others and consider fairly what they said. She thought about Adam's treatment of her, how he wanted to control her and feared her thinking for herself, and decided what the Serpent said must be true.

"So she began to fear Adam. But she was wise enough to allow him to perpetuate the idea of his dominion over her, in case he struck her too. God was pleased with his joke. It was always his way to turn a gift into something troublesome; just so with the gift of life for both of them. Eve could never give Adam the happiness he sought, and she knew that with him, she too could never be happy.

"Adam felt that his happiness was always just beyond what he wanted most – his power. Even at the times when Eve submitted completely to him, still he was unhappy because he knew that she was not being her true self. Yet when she was herself, he did not have the strength to accept her cleverness and so worked to make her believe she was weak so he at least did not feel challenged by her. It was a cycle with no end.

"Looking on, Lilith pitied Eve for the cruelty of God's trick. She watched as Eve sought among the creatures of the Garden for a confidante who could counsel her in her unhappiness. She found one – the same creature who had warned her of Adam's violence. He was a handsome creature, smart and subtle and charming, all the things Adam was not. And the creature fell in love with Eve, and promised he would do anything for her."

Here, Lissitch wipes his eye, as if a tear that Donitza could not see were about to drop. He looks to her and goes on:

"Lilith, seeing what was going on, broke her silence. She tried to warn Eve and Adam that if they carried on like this, without resolving their differences, there would be a disaster. Of course, neither would listen.

"So Lilith shrugged her shoulders, and accepting the terms of her divorce, went her own way. She was by now heavy with child and she gave birth to a beautiful daughter with hair as dark as the very night her mother was made from. Her daughters and their daughters had little to do with the sons of the Red Man, except that there were times when they could not help for a while to be together – because that was how they were made. To live together, to fall apart. And in the lives of the daughters of Lilith, whenever the Red Man came, there was invariably upheaval and trouble."

He sits silent a moment. Donitza waits for more, but it does not come. She is puzzled by it, since the story seems to go nowhere and leaves her dissatisfied at its lack of an ending.

"A pretty fairy story," Donitza finally answers in an attempt to dismiss it, her heart pounding as she speaks nearly stealing the voice from her words.

Her mind is racing. *Who is this Lissitch? What is he? Why is he here?*

Tears form as his story presses the buttons of emotion in her, a skilfully prestidigitated configuration of psychological vulnerability awakened. How could he know what this story would do to her? The elements within it –

The Red Man. The lonely woman with no father for her daughter. A life among the wild creatures and the night sky.

- It's too much. She takes a long-drawn breath that turns to a sob. She coughs to cover the sound of emotional surrender. Her throat aches.

"Well that is my story for you. Now in return, it is time for you to tell me yours," he says.

Somehow – she doesn't know how – his story causes her to tumble out her history. She speaks of her past, of her childhood in the heights, of magic and shared moments of secret knowledge. She speaks of the awe and wonder in her childhood, of the things she learned that no-one else knew – and of her loneliness, her otherness, her sense of apartness.

And then, with faltering voice, she speaks of the day her mother died. She grows angry. For with her last words to her, her mother told her that music would be her protection, that it would keep her alive. She goes through the scene over and over in her mind, replaying it and then comparing it to the last few days and the dark memory of assault and rape which she still has not fully processed, and that now presses on her with shocking reality.

She breaks down and reveals the voice in her head that speaks the accusation that has stayed with her all her life and made her play her violin. Honouring her mother's memory is an expression of her daughter's guilt.

Hot tears fall.

"Thirty seconds," she says through them. "If I had played for thirty seconds longer, she would have lived. The jet came in just too late."

Yet more spills out. Why does she play? – To keep that moment alive: the last moment she saw her mother. It is why her music is filled with hope and sadness all at once, as it freezes the moment in crystal air.

And now the final link to her mother is gone. With the violin's destruction, her protection is destroyed. But the truth is, she now knows it was a false protection. She fell and broke the violin *while* she was playing. Which means her mother's words about music providing safety were empty. She was *never* safe while she played. Her mother taught her nothing useful. Nothing acknowledged or accepted by those around her. She had made her different from everyone else, for no reason. When she looks back now she can see – it was all tricks and illusions. This is what her mother filled her life with. An old glamour: deceit.

She speaks of the time she later spent in the world of men. In transit areas and refugee camps. "There is no space for monk's hood and leopard's bane in the hard places of the world away from that mad woman's daydream," she says. "Pointless. A pointless otherness. Why? *Why?!*"

With rising anger she speaks of the fantasies that shape the world. There is no God that the Christians and Muslims speak of. There is no magic. There is nothing. Only the black emptiness that is life. No onwards, no *cycle of becoming* as she was taught. Just the end of everything in the snow.

Sobs wrack her, mucus streams, tears tumble.

Lissitch waits a long moment, sphinx-like, maintaining an amused objectivity at the creature before him, an ethereal luminescence stokes in his green eyes. He waits, counting his breaths, it seems, sensing the mood of the other. Waiting for the right moment.

Finally it comes.

"You know, apart from Adam, there is another Red Man?" He waits a moment longer as she lifts her face toward him. "He is greatly misunderstood." He pauses a moment and then goes on. "Some have said the greatest trick the Devil played was making man doubt his existence. Others say that the greatest deceit God chicaned was tricking his angels into misunderstanding the nature of His rival."

He moves his hands quickly and pulls a flower from the empty air. It is Devilbane, she notes in bewilderment as, with a deft move, he vanishes it again.

"There are things you see and things you don't. The places where you focus your attention will predict which of those things you notice," he says. "You thought you saw a flower appear from nowhere and disappear into nothingness because I distracted your attention. When you look in one place, you forget the things that are more important that you saw in another place."

He does it again. Infuriatingly, he lifts the flower from the ground where she cannot be quite sure it did not rest before, and throws it into the air. It vanishes as it leaves his hands. The surprise on his face surprises even her, and despite herself, a childish smile lights her face. She feels a rising sensation – a tingle in her stomach that is half way between fear and excitement, which rises upwards with a heady rush. It falls away at his next words.

"You remember only part of your story because that is where your attention lies. But there is another story you have forgotten that shows you your mother did not lie..."

He raises his hands placatingly in reaction to her flash of anger.

"She told you you would be safe. Despite everything, you are still safe. Only when you give up believing you are safe do you make yourself vulnerable. But *safe* does not mean *same*. Time does not stop. Did your mother never tell you that? That somehow the ice must crack?"

She is taken aback. Her head is swimming. Yes, she concedes to herself, in her own way, her mother did say this. He goes on:

"You have something in your mind. A film that plays over and over again. It is a terrible film filled with terrible things. But there will come a time you shrink it to nothing and flick it away with your fingernail. That way time for you will begin again."

He shakes out a raisin once more onto the palm of his hand. His eyes are narrow slits, his face shows no emotion. There is only a rhythmic speech that she hears above her hushed breath. He speaks low now, confiding.

"You are not just your mother's daughter. You are a woman of your own, too. You can make decisions, go beyond what your mother told you to do. You can be whoever you want to be. Let go the weight of your past and fly to your future. You can take charge. All it takes is a work of imagination to begin to be great."

Donitza feels the impact of his words resound through her body. They leave her disoriented, afraid, angry, unsure.

"Without her, I don't know what to do – " she says, and breaks off, her voice cracking. Finally, she adds: "What am I supposed to do?"

He waits yet another moment, until his words have maximum effect.

"You can think of your imagination as a creature that leads you in certain directions. You cannot always guess its motive. Perhaps it will lead you to destruction. Perhaps it will take you to something that will help you. In the end it is for *you* to decide what your imagination vouchsafes you. You are your own woman. So, it is up to you to decide whither you will go."

Her eyes ache. She puts her hand over her forehead and wipes them, clearing away the tears that have risen in her for the last few minutes, the tide now dropping away, her island of self re-emerging from the salt water. As she closes her eyes to order her emotions, he speaks six words that make the hairs on the back of her neck stand up.

"Do you believe in the Devil?" he asks.

In the silence after those words, she thinks she hears a skirl of laughter echo in her ears.

"What?"

She looks up sharply to the chair where he was seated. He is gone, with only the flower left on the chair.

She steps quickly to the landing. A cold wind is blowing up the stairs from where the door stands wide open. Celia is blinking up from the hallway, as confused as the young woman who looks down at her.

*

In the icy night air the girl looks down on the figure at her feet, a tumult of emotions turning inside her. Fear. Desperation. Loss. All harden to a numbing cold as she tries to take charge of herself and the situation she finds herself in. Her emotions are night creatures that will tear her to pieces if she lets them. She must not lose control, and so she starts to create the icy cold within her: quelling the emotions, freezing them in their tracks, turning them to ice.

She watches the light dying in the soldier's eyes. From time to time he shifts in his delirium, calling out more words of the Ecstasy; each time the light she notes dies some more. She looks around her at the night air and the blue glow of snow and the ferns beyond the cave and she doubles back to her purpose.

She works with haste, studying the night sky as the constellation of Orion swings slowly around the Polestar in its hunt for the Bear. In a while the moment will be right, when the moon swings between the hunter and the hunted, lighting the shot. Even now, the bowman is tensing the string.

Full efficacy will then be transferred to the liquid she is bringing to the boil in the pan she found at the back of the cave. A heavy skillet that the soldier did not bring here, but perhaps was left by others hiding out years before. She sings, a low old song her mother taught her, and feels the vibration of the incantation imbuing the air around her with a gossamer lightness – a matrix – a network of interconnectedness that she imagines for a moment she can see: silvered, like a spider's web, connecting all things. Bubbles are releasing their grip from the pan's interior, moving upwards toward the moonlight, each a shimmering moon of its own. With haste, she stops her singing and steps over to the soldier. In her language she says to him:

"Come. You must come. Now. Sit. You must sit up."

She puts her hands onto the heavy webbing he is wearing, upon the gun belt and straps over his shoulders, grips tight and pulls. He murmurs a low groan and sobs and she lets go without moving him at all. She tries again, bracing herself against the floor more solidly, but she feels her feet slide backwards on the earth as she realises she does not have the strength.

She looks around her. A tool. A lever.

There is a gun in the corner of the cave by the entrance, snub barrelled and heavy. She takes hold of it, pushing the short stock into the ground by his back and pushing him toward the skillet.

Quickly, she tells herself. She must act quickly or the moment will be lost.

He opens his eyes to the dark figure standing over him. He sees the dark shape of a gun, feels its hard pressure on his back. He moves with lightning speed, pulling a knife from his boot and reaching up with the other hand. He takes her by the hair and she gives a short yelp as he pulls her head backwards lifting her chin to the night sky. The point pushes up, glinting in the moonlight toward the soft flesh above her throat. She is trying to look down at him, though her head is back and she catches the glinting movement. She tenses and gives a sharp inhalation, waiting for death.

It does not come. He is upright now and blinking at her, seeing her face a sheet of silver in the moonlight; she catches the fear and confusion in his eyes. Still held in his grasp, she points to the skillet, then gestures with a wave, too frightened to talk, her heart pounding and filling the air with noise.

He nods and releases her, then struggles across the floor until he is sitting by the skillet licked by flames from below. He lifts a billycan, waiting for her to dole what he thinks must be stew, saying a few words in foreign soldierese, a joke about her cooking, perhaps.

She puts her hand gently on his shoulder and takes the billycan from him. He waits, watches, puzzled.

Finally, with a short incantation she throws three leaves into the boiling mixture and pulls his hand to the water. The fingers are black and rotting, she can see that. She sings the words her mother taught her as she does so. He looks at her as if she is mad, but she nods to him as his hand hovers over the water. She looks up out of the opening of the cave. The moon picks out the shot for the hunter. The time is now or never. With a final thrust she plunges his hand into the water. He shrieks. She holds it under as a meteor streaks from the quadrant with Orion toward the Bear. The Bear is dead. Just as her mother told her.

The soldier is looking dumbfounded at his hand under the water. Pus-filled rotten flesh is falling away to reveal pink skin. She sings a further charm in the voice her mother taught her, then releases him. He pulls his hand from the water, looks at it for a moment in shock, then slumps backwards on the gravel.

She dowses the flames with the potion and, above the hissing, listens to the night for a few minutes. Silence all around. Satisfied, she turns to him. She has found among his kit a field dressing pack and now tears it open and administers a bandage. He looks up at the sky, breathes quietly, then turns his eyes to her in surprise. Outside, there is a movement in the bushes. A fox's thin snout peers from the ferns. The creature licks its lips. She picks up the soldier's knife with one hand, hefts a stone with the other and shoos it away.

*

The fox. Donitza pushes the door closed on the icebound street, after checking to see whether her visitor was still out there. He was not, nor was there a sign he ever had been. Closing out the street's lonely cold, she walks with purpose into Celia's kitchen. She follows an instinct as she reaches into the fridge, pulls out a rasher of bacon then steps into the snow by the back door. She needs time to think, and she needs a friend.

She sweeps her eyes over the garden. The cherub and stone cat look at her, but no fox steps forward from the bushes. She gives a low whistle and then a sung call, but still it does not come. After a while she throws the scrap of meat to the floor and decides she needs to see another friend, instead.

A question flashes in her mind. *The fox. What does it mean?* The question hangs, unanswered. She remembers the henhouse and the birds that died of fright. The savage deaths of other birds witnessed by the spatter of blood. She remembers the warm snout, the gentle way it clamped her sleeve in its teeth, pulling at her wrist and leading her through the woods. But what had it led her to on that terrible day? – *To a trap?* – *Or to a saviour?*

She feels lost in the woods again, with no trustworthy guide.

*

The morning after she heals his hand, the soldier wakes from deep sleep with bright eyes. During the night, she worked on his sleeping form, cleaned the wound in his shoulder, applied a bandage, covered him with the sleeping bag and piled whatever cloth she could find on him before taking up position in the doorway and falling asleep, slumped over his rifle. A connection. He is a connection. That makes him precious. She shoots her eyes to him, resting them on him unwaveringly.

Coming back to consciousness he remembers a shadowy exchange, the flitting dreams of delirium mixed with a dreamlike moonlight memory of pain and healing. He raises his hand before him, eyes the dressing secured by adhesive edging and then looks back to her. The colour has returned to his face. He speaks to her in her language:

"We need to get to safety."

With renewed energy, he stands, reaches in his camouflage backpack and pulls out a foil sachet.

After a breakfast of concentrated meats and sugary tea, he examines the radio with the bullet hole in it. He presses the buttons for a few seconds, then shrugs and packs it away.

"There is an Evac point some way from here," he announces after weighing their options. He speaks in her language, now his mind is clear. "It is a long and dangerous walk, but we need to get you to safety. We need to stay off the roads, go through the woods. Can you do it?"

She stands, hands him his gun and after a while, nods.

"I saw what happened," he says. "I saw it all. You are a witness to a terrible crime. When we get you to safety, you must tell them. Justice. It's vital you get justice. That they all do."

She nods to him again, satisfied with his words.

"I'll keep you safe," he says and smiles down at her, putting his hand on her head in reassurance.

She smiles up at him. *There.* He is her connection.

*

The night after his walk home with Donitza, Riley is at Vee's, expecting a knock on the door. He has been expecting it all the previous night and all this day after the fun he had with the Witch. He hasn't run as he thought he might. No. He's decided to face it. He can, after all, deny it. In the cold light of a courtroom, he can stand his word against hers – a vagrant foreigner. He will claim that she was up for it, that she was keen. They had got close over the days before. He'd even bought her a violin. She had invited him in. He'd just misjudged what he was doing. He thinks about it now, and realises he would have had her if he'd waited, anyway. But there's something about the act of control – fixing her drink – that turned him on, set him alight. *The court doesn't need to know that bit.* The story would run something like: *We had a good time, she liked being roughed up, and now, after the event she's regretting it.* It's nearly fifty / fifty. He can charm a jury. She's a foreigner without a penny. Twelve good British citizens. He knows whose side they'll be on.

Yet, no knock comes, and he sits in Vee's house quietly drinking. There is more of a change in him, the change Vee noticed before. A lethargy, like the way he is sometimes after he hits her, but more so. As if the life has started to seep from him. She is in the half world of knowing what he is and still wanting him. It is a heady mix, needing him and fearing him in equal parts, this dark presence in the room.

She can sense the restlessness underneath, the contained violence. She's had that before in her life, and wonders when the blow will come. She even considers the news reports she's seen of women defending themselves. *Provocation. Mitigation.* She wonders how much provocation it takes to legitimately defend yourself. The kids fear him, and he demands utter subservience when he speaks. She has realised, despite her earlier doubts, that she loathes him and wants rid of him, just as the boys do. And yet, somehow, she needs him.

Riley does not care about any of this. He only has one thought. *The Witch.* He cannot get the scent of her out of his mind. He had thought that in the recent angry spill of sex he would have raped her out of his consciousness. But no. She exists there, still. Haunting. Enigmatic. Detached.

A new enigma presents itself. No knock on the door from the police. The thought repeats itself insistently. *No knock. No knock.*

Why?

A consideration he hadn't entertained lights a lurid neon in his head. Perhaps she liked it. Did she need it, like they all need it? Is it that he is Riley and no-one will cross him? Is it that he has the luck of the Devil on his side, and he'll never be caught for his crimes? He laughs to himself and stands up. Vee watches him as he does so, not moving her face from where it is angled at the tv, but following him with wary eyes. He heads for the door, pulling on his leather coat as he goes. She is relieved at his going, and then has a pang, wondering when he'll be back.

*

The night wraps cold fingers around him the moment he steps out the door. Her house is round the corner, 400 yards from where he stands and he walks along the arctic streets, his boots creaking on the snow compacted to ice, the dull orange of the streetlights deceiving the eyes to imagined warmth. He turns the corner, walks the street and thinks he sees a man, a slim figure, standing at her doorway, looking up at her window. Riley steps sideways into the cover of a garage entrance, alarmed. Who is he? A police officer, maybe? The one who is going to knock?

He swears to himself and laughs at his own jitters. He can't get her off his mind. The bloodless sinking feeling in his gut like a dull throb is what? Guilt? No. He doesn't feel guilt. He does bad things and he doesn't feel guilt.

He remembers the night when he discovered that was true. Stealing a boat. Breaking the chain on a yacht's tender on the shore by striking it with a rock. A mad scrabble. A plastic builder's bag he found on the foreshore that was once hoisted by a crane from the back of a truck before being discarded. Himself, tying a bundle with swift fingers, tight and then tighter.

He sees himself rowing out across the muscular flexing of the sea, carried out on the tide under the giant night sky, feeling alone, a transgressor, imagining himself rowing out beyond the world to the darkness beyond and becoming a part of it. *Pull, pull.* The line of the seafront disappearing as he looks backward, the low shadowed dilapidation of the radar buildings and the old Navy firing range shrinking to nothing.

Steering in the direction of the old navigation tower, out into the deepwater shipping lane. At one point going utterly still while a yacht nightsails past him where he sits on the water in the blind side of the moon. Farther off, the immense wall of a container ship pushing through the water.

He looks along the street again. The thin man is looking up toward him as if he knows he is there. Riley watches the man watching him. He sees him raise a hand, in salute to him, or thinks he does. The next moment the figure steps backwards across the road into a doorway opposite as her door opens. The Witch steps out, pulling a coat around her. Carrying her violin case strapped on her back she heads down the road in the direction of the sea. He can't stop himself. He follows her, half an eye on the recessed doorway where the thin man retreated. He expects to see him there. But no. No one is there. He must have gone inside, he thinks.

After he passes, a fox trots out from where he looked and follows him along the road, a flattened shape in the yellow light.

*

As the girl treks with the soldier through the snow, she begins to think he is perhaps more than a man. He has an instinct for the track they should take, and an almost supernatural knowledge of where enemy troops may be. They move quickly through the woodland, his strong arms lifting her when she flags and slinging her over his shoulder. She clutches him with a desperate tightness and there are times that he has to loosen her young arms to prevent her choking him, or hitting him with the violin case she refuses to let go of.

At other times he puts her down in the snow, checking a map against a compass and measuring the terrain with his eyes. During one such time, he grows impatient. Checking their current position against his watch, he speaks to her with a heavy foreign accent: "The going is too slow. We need to be over the next hill in one hour."

He considers her slight frame and his training. He should leave her, but he cannot. He saw her mother die. She is the witness. He tells her so. *One day there will be a reckoning.* That, he promises her. *A payback for these men who did this. But first we need to get across the valley and over the next hill.*

To their right, as he checks the route, the sound of a sputtering engine clatters against the trees, then dies out, replaced by a soft silence. He ducks through the bushes and comes to a road, where he spies a young soldier, a local militia member of perhaps 17 in an open-backed truck, pulled over to drink coffee from a flask. After a whispered instruction, he sends Donitza out. She wanders from the bushes, and stands by the roadside in front of the truck, looking up expectantly at the boy with his soft doughy face.

He freezes, and for that moment she sees in his face a boy caught out by an angry mother while stealing a few minutes' rest. He downs his coffee quickly and prepares to go out and investigate this little creature. Simultaneously his door is wrenched open and a strong pair of hands pulls him from the cab. The soldier holds the boy down pointing a gun into his face.

"Stay," he says, and gestures Donitza to climb in.

He keeps the gun on the boy while he relieves him of the pistol in his holster and pockets it. He is about to shoot the boy, but stops himself because he thinks of his young companion. Again, he says, "Stay," and moves back toward the truck, keeping the gun trained on him all the time. Donitza is watching them through the window in the cab.

The soldier climbs in beside her and turns the key in the ignition. The engine groans but will not start. He tries again. The third time he tries, a pistol comes through the open window of the cab. Another gun. The boy had another gun hidden in his boot.

"Get out," the boy says.

The boy is not a trained soldier but a hastily recruited child keen for adventure, wanting to play his part in great events. That is why he stands too close to be out of the destructive orbit of this other man whose life is killing and risk. The soldier snatches at the pistol, but the boy at least has reflexes honed on a football pitch and pulls back instinctively. As he does so, the soldier ducks and thrusts against the door, smashing it into the boy's face. The boy's hand tightens and a shot resounds metallically in the close space of the cab. The soldier snatches the gun with a deft and fluid action and turns it on the boy. With a single movement the bullet knocks the back out of the boy's head. The soldier kicks the body into the bushes and pulls the door shut with fierce precision. This time the engine starts.

Thirty seconds along the road he turns to Donitza. Blood is trickling from her pale mouth and she slides down her seat, her body jamming against the door.

*

On the island city, the snow is turning to an icy rain.

Donitza remembers it all like a dream. She shivers and pulls her coat tighter around her as she walks through the darkness.

She remembers how the bullet passed through her body with unexpected dullness, making time slow down around her. A deep throbbing pain that pulsed with the beating of her heart, her breathing weakened: each draw and release suffused in pain. She had been cold just a few seconds before, but now her body was filled with sickly heat. Sweat drenched her. She remembers it all. She has the mark on her skin over her ribcage. She looks at it sometimes in the mirror, running her musician's fingers over the scar tissue with a distant look in her eyes.

After that shot, the world descended into a flicker of chance images, pictures shuffled by the twitch of a cardsharp's thumbs.

A remembrance of flight: the truck hurtling along a pine-lined road. A checkpoint. Ramming the truck through it. Him grabbing her and jumping from the cab. His scrabble to reach the evacuation point. Gunfire peppering the truck with bullets. Crashing through woods at the base of a hill as he scrambles upwards with her in his arms. Her screams of pain growing weaker as they climb. Desperately clinging to him, and desperately, too, clutching her violin case.

They jolt up a loose scarp into thicker woodland. She is aware in some distant part of her brain that they are being hunted. She imagines hearing wolves baying around her. In a clearing she sees the afternoon sky above her, the pale moon appearing like her mother's face, smiling down on her. Benign. Serene. Detached.

Donitza surfaces from these remembrances, her hair soaking. She has arrived at the mound of snow that conceals the Fort. She sees through the hole in the metal doors a light inside. Rather than try to reason with him, she circles the Fort and climbs up, over the railings as she did once before, walking along the old parapets in the ice cold rain before sliding down on the other side, landing in an uncomfortable heap.

Eddy hears her and looks at her from the door of his workshop.

"NO!" he shouts. "I said no."

She dusts herself off and comes toward him. He turns from her as she approaches and she catches a glimpse of panic. When she enters the workshop, he is standing in the corner of the room, rocking from side to side and moaning, penned in by her slim frame at the door.

"Eddy, what is it?" she asks, coming closer in the room's warm sterile brightness. "Why won't you see me?"

He stays like this, agitated, rocking and moaning and she steps closer still, putting her hand on his shoulder. He responds with a violent shove back, and as he does so, she sees the bruising on his face. His hand is bandaged, she notes.

"Keep away!" He pushes her again, barging her backwards out of the door with surprising strength, shouting for her to go. She loses her footing and slips on the floor. He begins a panicked assault, arms flailing, breathlessly shouting. A rain of slaps falling on her head. "Go! Go!"

She scrabbles upright on the ground, her hands raised to ward off the flailing slaps. She makes a decision. With a sharp kick, she sinks the toe of her boot into his groin. He goes down, inhaling painfully, gasping at the air, his eyes bulging behind his glasses. His mouth makes a silent shout, frozen in such a perfect circle that she almost laughs out loud at the impression she has of a landed fish struggling to breathe.

She sits next to him on the disturbed snow.

"Breathe," she says. "Just breathe in deep. Yes, like this." She takes a deep breath herself. "The pain will pass."

He says nothing for a while, blinking at the sky. The rain has thinned now to a few spots and a deeper chill is filling the air. After a minute longer, he turns his surprised eyes to her and says, "A cup of tea. I could do with a cup of tea."

She ruffles his thinning hair and starts to laugh at the whole scenario. He blinks up at her forlornly as he watches her walk to the workshop, where the kettle waits, white and plastic.

Ten minutes later they are in electric fluorescence, drinking the infusion that makes so many of the English function. After a few minutes' uneasy silence, she opens the violin case, pulls out the broken instrument and says:

"Do you think you can fix this?"

He gives a stifled yelp at the sight of it, remembering the notes flying up in the street, the echo in the tunnel where the matchstick Guildhall rests. Tears needle his eyes.

He lifts it and eyes the broken neck more closely. "I... No... Toys, I do toys." He puts it down again and pulls paper kitchen towel from a roll on the windowsill and wipes his eyes, gently dabbing around the lurid bruising.

"What happened?" she asks.

He looks a question and she responds with a finger pointing in a circular motion to her own face as a mirror to his bruising: "This."

He sips on his tea a while longer, his head down. The icy rain has stopped completely and the night is clearing. A frigid breeze spills over the fort before sweeping on its way and goosebumping through the town.

"It was... Riley," he says, noticing her fist tighten at the syllables. "He saw you come here. He doesn't like you... being my... friend."

"Why didn't you tell someone?"

"No one believes what I say." He remembers kids jeering *special needs* at him at school; teachers run too ragged to intervene. *Authority.* He will not go to the police because they, too, are authority and are unreliable. Besides, there is something else.

"He said he would kill me. And you."

She laughs at the words. "Did he, now?"

She considers the threat contemptuously. *Kill someone. How easily such a threat works on a mind formed in a world where killing is not commonplace.*

"He's a bully. I've seen his type before. They are so boring in how identical they are. Him! Kill someone?" She lets out a contemptuous breath, half a laugh, half a spit of disgust. He had to drug her to overpower her, that weakling. "He couldn't kill anyone."

Eddy struggles with a thought, groping around in his mind to find the strength he needs.

"He did it before," he blurts out, pausing afterwards to see if retribution falls on him from somewhere unseen. Then, feeling relief that none has come, he adds: "Killed someone, I mean."

She tenses and studies his blank face with its eternal look of surprise. He is trying to avoid her eyes. His are troubled and filled with tears. His words hang over the two friends, as if they, too, have been frozen by the shock of what they convey.

"When?" she asks eventually, a pain in her stomach, her breathing tight. "Who?"

*

Riley remembers the night. That hot night when he couldn't sleep and slipped from the house. Out along the seafront, past the old sea wall on his left. The sea-anglers were gathered at the water's edge, spending their night stories in the dark or sitting in the silent companionship of escaped domesticity. They were all waiting. For what? A hope-filled twitch that was or wasn't a bite? Waiting for the *could have been* that comes from a fisherman's story, that glittering social coin?

The moon was a sliver in the sky, a *Muslim moon* he calls it. But it was also the town's moon. Near its crescent horns hung a bright star. A satellite looking down from on high, as likely to be watching for transgressors as relaying banalities with digital exactitude.

He walked to the swimming baths at the eastern end of the front, where his dad once told him war heroes trained. His dad. He felt sleep drain from him further. He watched the black night and the water and imagined what it is like to disappear beneath the waves, feeling the water accept you.

As he sat there alone in his thoughts, she came down to the shoreline, having picked her way here too because it was away from the anglers. Her movements were all lightness and grace. He'd watched her since they were kids. She was so beautiful. So smiling. They had been friends on the street – not close – but friends of sorts.

He remembered them playing. She was older than him by a few years. He would watch her as she talked with her friends, and her friends would nudge her and laugh at him. He remembered looking after her receding outline as she carried schoolbooks to her house. He'd wanted her even then, just to get that closeness – physical contact, that comes in so many forms. Love. Violence. All the same. He had always wanted her but never got her. Now, here she was, a silhouette against the starlight. Tall and slim and beautiful. Always stylish.

He had seen her a few months before in her cableknit dress that was like a body stocking. He was deeply impressed by that look. It accentuated her shape, and he had sought out her skin in the gaps in the pattern. Now she was in a summer dress and carried a towel in her hand. As he watched, she slipped out of it and into the warm sea, plashing naked in the starlight. No swimsuit. At 2 a.m. the night was clothing enough, he supposed.

When she came out, he was standing holding the towel for her. She was unabashed, and when he offered her a little pill – Molly for Janey – she said *yes* and laughed. It was, he told himself, inevitable that after all this time they would get together. He couldn't believe his luck. After she took the pill, that's when he made his move. That naked woman half lit by a sliver of moon, his fingers in her hair, she half laughing, then half shouting. His energy out of control made him move too fast.

When she stood again after he had forced her she was angry and crying. The MDMA hadn't even started to take effect, he realised. If it had it would have been okay – just another event in the flux of high experiences, which they would have laughed off later. So he thought. But he'd timed it wrong and now she rose and skittered away, naked on the stones that slipped beneath her beach shoes.

"You won't tell." He'd gone after her with those words, the tone of his voice shifting from commanding to pleading. "You won't tell?"

She carried on walking. He took hold of her arm and she kicked him ineffectually in the shin with her light shoes. Furious, he pushed her. She scrabbled for balance on the stones, falling backward, her body in full descent stopping with a single impact, her head jerked upwards as it hit the corner of a concrete block left 75 years before by a contractor for His Majesty's Navy in time of war.

After that, she didn't move.

He sees the image over again. Her, falling backwards, reaching up to the air. Scrabbling to take a grip. And falling. Falling backwards. Arms outstretched.

Riley remembers it all. The silence after that crash except for the lapping of the waves on the stones. A few moments in which he assessed the situation coldly. He had penetrated her, and now she was dead. She had bruising, MDMA in her stomach that he'd given her and his semen in her belly. He knew enough about the way the police would see this. *It was just a bit of fun gone wrong*, he told himself and believed it – but knew they wouldn't see it that way. That's when he decided to act. A smashed padlock, a yacht's tender, a bag. The body weighed down with stones and deposited far out in the sea channel. Even if they found her it would be years. Nothing to link her to him.

At sea, far far out he had pushed the heavy bundle over the side. The evidence travelling in a sinking builder's bag to the fishes and the crabs. *In the sea. The black, black sea.*

Now, as he stands outside the fort in the darkness, listening to the Idiot speak to the Witch, he knows his secret is under threat. He hears the Idiot describe how he was fishing on his own, away from the others, saw it all and said nothing. Trouble. The Idiot thought he would be in trouble if he told. And he knew Riley could kill, so he'd kept quiet all these years.

Riley hears Donitza's voice rise up, astounded and unbelieving. "You should have said. You should have said," she repeats. Then after a pause, she adds. "We have to say something now. Both of us."

Trouble breeds trouble, Riley supposes with an indifferent shrug. The lethargy he was weighed down by has gone from him now. Instead, an animal instinct has kicked in. Neither has spoken to anyone else, yet. Only they know.

The first Donitza knows of his presence is Eddy's panicked shout. She spins to catch a dark movement beside her and an explosion of light that sends her giddied to the floor, vaguely aware of a commotion around her.

*

Commotion around her. Her eyes are dim as the blood pulses from the bullet wound, despite the soldier's hurried pressing of a field dressing. She is floating outside herself as he lays her gently by a rock where there is bare earth in the wind shadow. He is looking up at the blue sky, and then down at his watch. A signal. He needs to make a sign on the ground to confirm he is there, and he runs into the trees around them, then emerges after a few seconds, pulling two long branches behind him. He runs out on to the open snow and throws them down. As he does so, the staccato of machine gun fire breaks the silence.

Now she is up, moving, drifting. She is walking on the snow without making a mark. She has become a creature of air and ice, she realises. She dances on the drifts, playing contentedly as she watches the soldier running to cover, the snow sputtering up around him.

She sees him look down at the ground by the rock where he laid her on the earth. There is something lying there, she can see, a bundle of rags. Briefly interested, she watches him stand over it, sees his body sag in a gesture of defeat. Snow flies into the air like confettied winter accompanied by the echoing peal of machine guns. She watches from a distance, seeming with each breath further away. He leans over the bundle and works on it – pushing down in quick movement. He even leans close to the bundle, kissing it.

"Funny man," she thinks. "What a funny man."

A figure emerges from the trees and walks toward her. Her eyes light up with recognition.

"Look Mama! The snow. Look at the snow!" She says, holding her hands out on either side at the flurry of feathers around her. Everything seems so new, so beautiful, to have a dimension she has never experienced before.

Her mother gives her a warm smile as jubilant Donitza dances to her and takes her hand. "I love the snow, Mama!" she says.

Her mother kneels and hugs her.

"You must go back, Sparrow," she says to her daughter. "Fly back to the man."

"But Mama, look at the snow!"

There is a whirlwind around them now. A blizzard spinning snowflakes into a vortex that makes it difficult to see beyond their cocoon of ice.

"Mama, isn't it beautiful!"

Her mother straightens her arms and faces Donitza in the whiteness.

"Yes. It is beautiful." She grows serious. "Now listen to me. A final lesson for you. The snowflake is the pearl of the air. It starts with the tiniest mote of dust which is warmer than the icy air around it. The snowflake gathers around the imperfection at its heart, stretching out tendrils, the arms of a structure – to make something delicate and beautiful. It is the same with the pearl, be it freshwater or salt that forms in the heart of the oyster around a grain of dirt. Its imperfection is the source of its beauty."

Donitza can hardly hear her now. The roar is so loud it is drowning her voice. Her mother speaks more urgently, spilling out the lesson with a rush of words.

"This is how it is with music, too. It will be born from the grain of dirt in your soul and it will be beautiful. Imperfection is virtue. This is why the men with crosses and crescents start from the wrong place." She takes Donitza and hugs her close to her bosom. "Goodbye, my Sparrow. Remember, your violin is your protection."

The vortex whirls around her. The soldier is now where her mother was, standing in a white maelstrom. He picks her up and runs to the helicopter that hovers a few feet over the evacuation point. Troops on board lay down covering fire – machine guns bark into the blizzard.

He pushes her into the arms of a medic and begins to scramble in. A panic seizes her and she shouts desperately, despite her weakness.

"My violin," she screams, tears streaming down her face. "My violin!"

The soldier stops. The others on board are shouting something at him, filled with anger and impatience. But he understands, she realises. He was the peacekeeper who called in the airstrike that saved her and the other villagers. He saw her mother die. He disappears back into the snow. She knows he is safe. They are connected. He is her connection.

There is a brief wait. The soldier returns, running with his head down. He is holding the violin case and has a victorious look on his face. He jumps in and stumbles forward as the 'copter rushes upwards in a roar of air and noise. As it banks to rush away, she sees the sign he left on the ground. Two branches in the shape of a cross.

In the roaring noise she is aware of movement on the other side of the cabin, where medics are kneeling. She looks to them, instinctively afraid at the way the soldier stumbled. He is lying on the cabin floor and medics are working on him. Then one of them turns away, shaking his head. As he moves, she sees the soldier looking toward her. In the middle of his forehead is a red hole the size of her fist where a bullet has passed through his brain.

*

In the room of fluorescent light, she opens her eyes and feels a searing pain in her head. She was knocked unconscious, she realises, after a few seconds of disorientation. A commotion outside comes to her ears and she totters up unsteadily to the door. A shriek flies up as the crescent moon breaks from torn clouds above.

From the doorway she can see Riley rampaging through the village. Beneath his boot, the Post Office shatters into ragged pieces, then the butcher, the baker, the candlestick maker. Neat rows of miniaturised 1950s pastoral idylls are flattened in swift, savage succession. Eddy, sitting on the floor, is staring with blind eyes, patting the ground to find his glasses. As another house cracks, he gives up the search, stands and rushes blindly at Riley, who effortlessly bats him to the ground, cruelty burning in his eyes.

Riley inhales and considers Eddy for a moment, then jumps on his stomach knocking the wind from him, leaving him gasping. His boot scuffs in the snow and a clank reveals a metal chain used as a low fence to stop visitors walking on one part of the village. Riley kicks at the post it is attached to and whirls the chain for a moment, a magic circle in the air.

He moves toward Eddy with his hands out, ignoring the shorter man's attempts to fend him away and gathers him up in his arms. Both of them slip in the struggle and Riley sits on the snow with Eddy on his lap, Riley's strong arm locking across his body, resisting Eddy's frantic efforts. As Eddy weakens, Riley wraps the chain around his neck.

He tightens it.

Eddy's eyes bulge, his face a red strain of frustration and anger that eventually succumbs to despair.

Riley tightens the chain more and Eddy's movements start to slow. Too late, his hand dropping down by his side finally finds the glasses he sought.

Donitza feels black rage rising inside her. A destructive hatred she has felt only once before. She is moving on instinct now, anger animating her body so she has no sense of control. With thought absent, she picks up the nearest object to hand and runs silently through the snow. Riley hears her at the very last second, turning to see the shape of the Witch, tall and lissom, swing the violin case into the side of his head. He sprawls sideways onto the snow and she strikes again as he tries to raise himself up on one elbow. The third strike sees the violin case break and spill its contents on the snow beside his splayed form.

She goes to Eddy, kneeling to unwind the chain from his neck. She shakes him. He opens his eyes and smiles weakly at her, then swivels his head to where Riley lies. He says:

"Is he dead?"

Donitza shrugs.

"I don't think so." Then with a rising wave of sadness and relief she says: "I thought I'd lost you." She cries hot tears that fall on his jacket or tumble on the snow, until a rising sense of panic scatters through him. He struggles out of her arms and totters to his feet, not sure what to do in the grip of this emotion. Finally, he says, agitatedly, in the absence of other words:

"Do you want some more tea?"

She sits back on the snow for a second and laughs at the absurdity of this Englishman and his tiny world.

"Yes, Eddy, I want some more tea."

Then the mirth dies in her eyes. She gestures the prone figure of Riley. "But first, help me move him."

They approach him timidly, like children who have sneaked into their father's room to play a prank. Only when they see he does not respond do they pull up the courage to drag him to the tunnel where she played for Eddy that first night. Closing the iron gates, they padlock him in.

Once it is done, Eddy walks to the workshop and Donitza goes back to the wreck of her splintered violin case.

Strewn on the snow, keepsakes from her mother have spilled from the lining. Paper packets, neatly folded small brown envelopes, each labelled with an astrological sign. She sees the image in her mind. Her mother, years before knowing danger was coming, meticulously preparing these spells and raw materials, hiding them inside the case's lining. Tools she might one day need.

She remembers watching her mother's handiwork, oblivious that she was preparing the packets for her. Inside are dried herbs, flower heads, amulets, powders, runes. She snatches them up, blind to the present world as her mind aches with questions and memories. She remembers her mother's voice. "Your violin is your protection."

*

Protection. Images rush in.

Arriving at the transit camp among a crush of bewildered humanity, she is handed into the care of a nun who tries to coax her into speaking. She will not speak. Not to one whose head is filled with the legends that fuelled so much hatred and murder. She will not talk to her of the things she has seen, but absorbs the suffering of humanity around her in the abandoned world. She hears talk of retribution, and one day, even of trials.

Nor will she speak to the men who come to her and ask her about her ordeal, though she knows they suspect her silence is her testimony. Who can she trust? Who will accept her? Her connection is gone.

Another face. This time, the mild face of a woman who came to gently question her. Donitza resolutely refused to go back over the ground she had covered so desperately to escape. Perhaps she might even conjure up once again the evil that was done to her. Perhaps if she trusted this woman then something terrible would happen to them both.

What did she tell her? What *could* she tell her when the U.N. investigator asked her for her story? Why would she not speak? She understands now. Because in all trust lies the seed of betrayal.

The summer before the attack, in a trip to the village, she had been cornered by old Radek, while her mother sought provisions.

After his wife died, old Radek had for a while been close to Donitza's mother for the little acts of kindness she had shown him. Once he even told the girl: "Your mother is a remarkable woman. She helped me when I was at my lowest - lifted me till I could stand on my own two feet."

Radek was right. Her mother was a healer. She always had been, and he experienced the power of her healing influence when his neighbours grew tired of his tears and she still stood by him, guiding him steadily back to the world his wife had left.

But on the day she was remembering, he had changed. The whole village had grown tense, uneasy, watchful. He was drunk, tottering down the street, seeming to wrestle with a walking stick, his wild eyes seeking an object on which to bleed his anger.

"You there. You! I haven't seen you in church. Are you sure you are on the right side of the river?" The old man waved his arm at the minaret piercing the blue sky on the far side of the town's concrete bridge.

Because Old Radek had spoken with her kindly in the past, she ignored her mother's warning: "Don't talk with them, now. Some of them think an idea more precious than a man."

"As you know, Radek, Sir, I live up there. Above the valley."

She pointed with a straight sunbrowned arm above the scarp to where she could just see her mother's hut clinging to the mountainside.

Radek straightened for a moment, realising he was being listened to. *Unusual.* His particular obsessions had so worsened since he'd lost his son in an accident – such a shock after his wife's loss – and this time even Donitza's mother had been unable to lift him from his grief.

He spilled his anger wherever he could. Nowadays, few listened as he rehearsed how a Muslim driver had braked too late when his drunken son stumbled from the night-tide roadside. "Muslims. It was the bloody Muslims..."

For Radek, that half second had broached a bottomless cask. Troublemakers in the church had filled a font with his grief, a stagnant pool of resentment through which he was born again into hatred. He hobbled close to Donitza, pushing his lined face close to hers, inspecting her.

"Not a Muslim then?" Donitza shrugged. "No. What are you up to, up there? Your mother teaching you about the Devil?"

"No, Sir."

She had been told by her mother that some of the men here had been sent mad with their beliefs. The tension had certainly grown worse over the last year; outsiders, with their agendas, coming in, working on grievances, stirring up distrust. Old Radek was one of the fruits of their labour. The change in the old man surprised her.

Donitza couldn't resist repeating her mother's warning, as if in response to a need to put things in their place.

"My mother tells me that some of the men in the town are mad, now. Are you?"

A slim teenaged boy in the street who was watching the exchange laughed. Old Radek was not amused and hopped from one foot to the other, pointing his stick at her.

Then he pulled himself up to his full height and this time made the sign of the cross on himself, kissing the silver crucifix around his neck.

"You see this? This is the only way. What do you do up there? Does she teach you to mix poison... show you how to talk with birds and beasts?" his imagination ran on. "Where is your father? Did she poison him? Are you the Devil's daughter?"

"I told you, I do not know who the Devil is."

He brought his face level with hers.

"Playing the innocent? I don't think so. The Devil looks after his own, they say," he added, glancing up at a movement in the drenching sun.

It was her mother. Marching up to him from the doorway to the store, she pushed her finger into the base of his throat where the collar bones join to form a notch. With this simple manoeuvre the old man started to choke. He stepped back, coughing and directed his ire at the woman who towered over him.

"Walking with animals by moonlight, mixing potions. What are you doing, up there?"

Her mother said nothing for a while, not moving, looking levelly back until the man finally flinched under her glare.

"You will not threaten my daughter," she said with a clear tone. "You will not do that. She is protected."

*

In the workshop, she throws down the packets on the table and pores over them, studying each, confirming what she suspected. The words and symbols reveal the packets are steeped in spells, charms, blessings and an injunction: to come to Donitza when she needs them.

The energy pulsing through them causes her hands and arms to tingle. Involuntary tears film her eyes as she senses her mother's influence. Weeks, months of preparation, drying in the moonlight and sunlight, incantations, music – and her own playing. All these have shaped the virtues in these herbs.

These are the protection her mother promised her. As the realisation grows inside her, Donitza comes alive with the memory of the craft her mother taught her.

She considers her past with fresh eyes. The long lessons in which her mother had spoken of the goodness that could be done with her knowledge. The injunctions to act in good faith, and not to taint her decisions with impulsiveness. To allow the magic to work from a place of good heart.

She hears her mother's voice again: "The werewolf has its home in the night and is cruel beyond compare. But even with him there are means to turn him. Shadow can only be cast by light. When you meet malice, seek to give it love. Do nothing from malice yourself. As the song grows out from a single note and can turn in any direction, so you can turn the shadow to light. You can be its counterpoint. Its transformation. The world is a broken world but you are not broken, child. Remain unbroken."

She considers Riley and weighs him. Can she turn him? Does she want to? Is it even possible?

She still wonders about her mother. Wisewoman or madwoman? Had her mother played conjuring tricks upon her like her strange visitor, Reynold Lissitch? Or had she really been creating deep magic? She sits on a stool by the workshop table, puts her hand to her cheek and considers for a moment, resting her head on her palm as she ponders.

"Were they lies she fed me, that now fill my memories of childhood? Or were they true?"

Eddy places a mug of tea by her and she tries to look backward again into her past for a clue. Did she dream it all? The spells her mother taught her? The good she must do, the dark she must avoid, the healing she must perform, the harm she must prevent?

She is distracted by a bellow from deep in the arched brick tunnel.

"You'd better let me out, you fuckers. *You have no idea what I'm going to do to you!"*

*

More of her childhood comes to her. The gaps are filling like the white spaces in a child's colouring book. A pattern that reveals itself to her.

Danger. Escape. Safety. Loss. Betrayal.
Danger. Escape. Safety. Loss. Betrayal.
Danger. Escape. Safety. Loss. Betrayal.

A few years later, not sure where to place her, the authorities left her in the care of a Catholic educational institution in Italy. She remembers the publicly aired smiles of the nuns, and her private terror at these women who controlled each and every minute of her life. An old place built of stone, with the scent of Vatican incense fused in the paint and the walls, lit with cold sunshine through glass, casting deep shadows from which brightly painted alabaster figures shot impassioned eyes heavenward for salvation.

Lessons were run by mechanical routine, and she spoke in class only when she had to. She made a friend. A mouse who sat on the wall in the courtyard in the sun, russet brown, thin faced with eyes that followed her. She noticed it watching her when she walked by, and between the prayers in the morning and the dull classes that left her feeling empty and heavy and filled with lifeless parables, there were breaks for the children to play.

She would grin at the mouse and it would stare back. Sometimes she felt as if they were conspirators. Over time, it really did become her friend. She trained it to come to her hand, where she would feel its trembling vulnerability. She held it sometimes, its impossible weightlessness a nothing that nevertheless projected soft, aspen warmth; a shock of otherness – the creature's delicate frame seemed to her to stand as a symbol for all life.

Sometimes she kissed it when she ran a delicate finger over its head and down its back. Holding it close to her face, she spoke with it, and imagined that it understood her. One day she told it the story of the Red Man and the Dead Man, and laughed as her mother laughed, and remembered a golden day in the sunshine on a hill, looking down on a village that soon would be burned to black bones.

When she was done, a hard hand grabbed her roughly by the neck, and she dropped the mouse, which scurried to safety, but continued to watch her as she was dragged away. She was marched to *Madre Superiora* and told by her accuser to tell her story again. The Madre looked down on her with hard, earnest eyes, and Donitza felt a shadow on her heart, and had a sudden remembrance of the dark-haired Captain on the mountainside in the snow. She froze and would not speak.

Thus, though she admitted to nothing herself, she was beaten with a cane after the nun related what she had said; she was told that God would punish her wickedness in the afterlife, as if somehow this cane and these bruises and tears were not enough.

That night, she said goodbye to her little russet mouse, gathered her violin from under her bed and ran away from the home, never looking back at the school's shadowy eminence that blocked out the stars.

*

She is looking at the packages before her and also not looking. She is feeling their presence and trying to recapture the elusive scent of her mother. Mother. Mater. The root of all matter. The matrix. The web that holds the world together. Is she there, in these herbs? Is this the reunion she has yearned after, for so long?

After she ran away, she played violin across the continent of Europe and never once sought to use the vital powers in herbs or speak the spells her mother gave her. What if she were beaten again?

Then, coming to rest in Spain a while, she made a friend. A boy whose eyes were so pretty, so black as if he were wearing kohl, that she thought him to be from another world. She stayed with him a while in the vast anonymity of Madrid, where it was possible for her to blend in, to play, to work as a waitress serving tapas in a bar, pulling drinks, flicking open pressured bottles and discarding buckled bottletops in a green plastic bin.

How comfortable was that little dream, those months of bliss! He was so different, so other, and one night she told him of the wolf in the night, of her mother, of spells of conservation, and of catching moonbeams. He was amused by it all.

"Una historia encantadora, hermosa," he told her, and laughed, and she took solace from that laughter.

The next night, she drew down from the sky a nightingale. She did it with song. The little creature had been singing lonely in the night, perhaps lost and taking shelter in a nearby tree. She called to it by singing from her window, and the bird came to her, resting on her hand, whistling back the song she sang. She had done it, too, by painting in the air the outline of the bird – something that hung radiant in the night, like a moonbeam.

The boy had stared with disbelieving eyes and suddenly afraid had said:

"Brujería!"

Witchcraft!

With a sternness forbidding contradiction, he assured her with hard face and calm voice that she would be punished by God for her sins.

Danger. Escape. Safety. Loss. Betrayal.

So, once again, she buried her memories under a layer of snow. Each and every time those memories tried to scrabble out from the avalanche she had used to trapped them, she ran. Always running, moving on so that the thing that was behind her would never catch her.

–

She stops in her long train of remembrance, exhausted, a wreck of emotions.

Now, here it all is: From that whiteness, the empty expanse of her childhood has at last been repopulated.

*

She is standing in the starlight at the mouth of the tunnel, looking in at him through the iron bars of the gate, undecided as to her path. He is posturing and swaggering, even with that growing welt on the side of his head. He looks an accusation as she stands before him, her hands behind her back.

"What the fuck is going on?"

She doesn't answer and he puts his hands on the bars, the frame giving a metallic rattle that reverberates down the tunnel. "You bitch. Let me out, or I'll –"

"What will you do?" she snaps at him, suddenly brave.

He is silent for a second at the force of her question, but he's *not having that.* He shouts her down, puffing and blowing and snorting, demanding to be let out, threatening her. "When I get out of here, just you fucking wait..." More pleas. More curses. She stands unmoving, watching him, this powerless figure, his face a contorted reddening mass of hate, until finally his anger blows itself out.

With inner calm, she says. "I could leave you there, if I wanted to."

"Sure, sure... you *could,*" he echoes, sarcastically. "But you won't. Of course you won't. You're going to be in so much shit. I promise you that. So much fucking shit."

She says nothing, looking at him with a cold, hard expression. She feels that she is the possessor of a cruel, unyielding energy – an energy that seeks to destroy in just the way he does. In the moondarkness she notices a flicker of recognition in his eyes.

Something strikes to his heart that he has not felt before.

He sees himself in a new light. Alone. Cold. Hungry. *Would she really? Leave him here?* She has reason to, he supposes. His bluster and rage empties out of him as he sees his situation from this different angle, and his shoulders drop.

"Look, let me out," he says, a wheedling tone entering his voice. "I know I hurt you – and your friend. It was just... to scare you a bit. A laugh. I overdid it. That's all. Come on... *mate.* I'm fine, now. You and me: we're fine."

Donitza considers him, studying his features, his helplessness; she feels a heady excitement at the power she holds.

She remembers another night again from long ago: sitting by the fire outside the hut in the moonlight. The grey wolf sitting at her mother's feet is distracted by the sound of movement in the darkness of woods on the far side of the road, outside the circle of light. Its body tenses as it raises its head with renewed alertness. Its eyes widen, bright, reflecting the yellow firelight, flames dancing in its eyes. With a swift movement it lifts itself and, head lowered, pads forward, a single point of concentration, its breathing seeming to have stopped, utterly silent. More movement in the woods. It advances toward it with no sound, a silent shadow beneath the moon, then with an explosion of power launches into a savage chase through the nightbound trees.

Her mother turns to her daugher with a gentle face: "The werewolf is at least predictable in wolf form," she says. "It is when it takes the shape of a man that you can never tell when the wolf will surface in him. Some have escaped the rhythm of the moon completely."

The moon. She feels its crescented presence. The timing is right tonight, she can sense it in her witch's blood, a current in her consciousness to which she hasn't responded for years. All this power and potential, bottled up. Hidden away, in case she drew attention to herself.

There was a full moon above while she was sitting with her mother in the firelight after the wolf ran off, *not like tonight,* she considers.

"The moon, we are the moon, my Sparrow," her mother had said. "Hecate is one of our names."

She could hear the crashing as the wolf broke through the undergrowth. Then after a few seconds of deeper silence, a high-pitched cry pierced the night. Something, an animal, screaming in the middle distance for a short moment; then silence.

"Our influence is everywhere and yet it is ignored. We lift the seas, we move the winds, we pull the tide in men's minds. Think of yourself in this way, my Sparrow. And remember, transformation is our essence. For the cycle of transformation applies also to her."

Her mother looked upward at the white disc, perfectly round above them. Her daughter's eyes followed hers to see *a look of sorrow on her face, her mouth open* – that is how the craters seemed to Donitza as she stared at the moon. *As if she is caught in a cry of pain.*

"The moon has three phases. It is the girl who is growing to womanhood. It is the full moon who is heavy with child and it is the old woman who carries deep knowledge and experience, even though she wanes."

"In your life you will be each of these. That is the Triple Goddess. And you must allow each to exist within you. Each in her time."

Donitza brings her eyes down from the moon and stands a while longer in thought before the iron gate. She steps in toward him.

"You say you will not hurt us?"

He smiles to himself, and hangs his head in submission, casting around to find the right words and remembering something one of his clients said a few days before.

"Of course I won't. Look, I'm not a bad person. Not really. Just – you know – like most of us. Trying to get by. Just getting by."

She steps closer so she is thirty centimetres from him. With a lightning movement he reaches out and takes her hair in a tight grip, tearing at the roots as he pulls her in, till her face is pressed against the hard iron of the gate, bruising her cheekbone with its cold edge. "Now, you're going to let me out, bitch! Come on. Give me the keys!"

Her hand comes out from behind her back and the silver glint of a blade moves in the light before it comes to rest, pressed hard into his skin over the carotid artery.

"You will let go," she says calmly, eyes slits like a cat's. "You will let go or I will cut your throat."

They stand like this for three seconds as he weighs whether she has the nerve to do it. He decides he is not quite sure, and lets her go. As he does so, her other hand darts forward through the bars and pulls a clump of hair from his head, jerking it out by the roots. As she walks back to the workshop he begins again his screaming. She hears him and now she knows what she must do. Her mind is made up. Yes, she is her mother's daughter and she will listen to her mother's teachings. But she is also her own woman, and she will cast her own magic. Something that proves to the world, to herself, how real her power is.

Her mind runs backwards and then forwards. She considers Lissitch's words and finds in them a clue that she will use – perhaps it is even guidance:

"You have a picture in your mind. A film that goes on over and over again. There will come a time when that picture shrinks away to nothing and you flick it away with your fingernail. That way you will live. Time will begin again."

She smiles to herself; a dark energy takes hold. She is driven now by potentials inside herself which are not completely under her control. She sees herself as an agent of the stars or the tides or the moon. She is connecting to the unseen axle and hub as she did once before. But this axis on which the world spins, it seems darker, more polluted than the one she experienced as a child. Yet its energy, the feeling it gives her... it is exhilarating.

In the tight workshop she says: "Eddy, I need to boil some water. Not in the kettle."

Her beauty seems terrifying to him now. This woman has a light in her eyes that is different from the sadness he saw before. Aggressive, cruel, imperious. Without a word he reaches down a pan from a shelf and places it hurriedly on the small stove in the corner.

"What you doing?" he asks, his words full of apprehension.

She turns to him, her face earnest, flat with seriousness. "Eddy, whatever happens tonight, whatever you see – we are friends. Do you understand that?"

He thinks about it for five whole seconds, the look of surprise on his face growing more surprised as the round plastic clock on the wall measures each second in turn.

He nods.

*

More memories come to her, this time from the formulary her mother impressed in her mind as a little girl. She remembers the powers inherent to the wedding of opposites, the virtues in metals, the branches of the tree of life and where each branch will lead in the creation of spells. She looks through the packets and is surprised to find among the herbs a different story from the one her mother taught her. For the packets contain not only substances that promote growth and healing, but those that weaken and destroy.

"These spells are forbidden to you to use, my Sparrow," she remembers her mother saying during one of the long nights of spellwork they spent together. "But I will show you how they are generated so you will know how to counter them."

Sternly she addresses her daughter as she lifts one of the plants ranged on the table before her and holds it up.

"With the virtues of these lords and ladies of the wood come great responsibility. They are imbued with a malicious power and you should be aware of their dark virtues in case you have to defend against them. So I will reveal to you the processes of Malign Transformation so that you know the steps to undo it."

Her mother lifts a glass phial containing a quantity of crimson powder.

"Firstly, Red Mercury, not born from the wood, but the offspring of the Earth and Saturnine Night. The King of Poisons, created by the Torment of the Metals." She pauses and circles the phial three times as she empties it. "In the creation of the malign transformative, the King must first be drowned in the Sea."

Donitza locates a packet of red powder and sprinkles it into the pan, making three circles as the powder turns the water to a deep blood red. Her mother's voice guides her.

"Once drowned, he must be made to live again in new and twisted incarnation. Upon resurrection, his virtues will not be entirely destructive, but they will be baneful and will corrupt all they touch. The resurrection is performed by the use of the following lords and ladies of the wood, the following words of power and the following harmonic form..."

Thus Donitza begins the construction of a potion, going through the packets to find Devil's Foot and mandrake, seeds of nightshade, comfrey, fly agaric and agrimony. All are there, as if her mother knew that one day she would need them. She takes the clump of Riley's hair and cuts it to tiny pieces and at the right moment adds it to the mix. "These spells are forbidden to you," her mother's voice tells her again, more insistently.

All the while Eddy watches her. Her face is alight with memories newly surfaced that she buried beneath the one memory that has ruled her by making her keep it at bay. Death. The remembrance of a moment at which her mother moved out of the world. How she buried her mother, but never acknowledged the burial. She is breaking free, an explosion of chaos and creativity ignited. She feels in some way stronger with each movement she makes, and the alarmed voice that tells her she is about to use her skills for a baleful, vengeful purpose she chooses to ignore.

That, after all, is the voice of those who live in a binary world, hating each other across a divide. She is above this. Her mother was too, and that is why her warning is hollow. *My mother didn't want her child able to use these dark powers so young, that's all*, she tells herself. *If I was never meant to use this power, then why show me? And why leave me this legacy?*

She understands this in the same way that she understands the insight Lilith must have possessed. From above the Earth Lilith could see the two-dimensional thoughts of Adam and, later, his children, plodding on the ground below her. She was a creature of the night sky. She was different, always indifferent to the rules of the people below.

In her heightened mood, Donitza sees beyond the world of representation and interpretation to the other world, the one devoid of morals, devoid of history, devoid of good or of evil. The world of the Ecstasy that was the energy at the beginning of time. As the malign chemicals strike her nose the glimpse into eternity makes her gasp.

In a moment the vision is gone. She works on, a devil in human form, and Eddy watches with misgiving plummeting through his soul. Finally, as the night grows old and the ingredients and incantations work to completion, she is ready. She is transformed now as she sings a charm over the bubbling pan and gingerly pours the hot liquid into a cup. She is another being now. The night embraces her, fits her perfectly, wraps around her like a cloak. She applies kohl to her eyes and other powders from the packets to her face, to become one with all the priestess queens of her mother's line who have gone before her. She is a symbol, an archetype, no longer a human being.

Thus she heads into the night.

Riley is sitting in the tunnel, shivering as she approaches. He sees her coming toward him, the steady confidence of her walk, the inscrutable look on her face: entranced. She is no longer a girl or a young woman, he senses without words, but a Fury, a cruel spirit incarnate.

She breathes calmly. The hub and wheel she represents now is utterly different to the one she experienced before as a girl. Now she is in command of the Wheel of Fortune, a spinning wheel on which the threads of lives are spun and gathered and cut. Riley is at its rim and will be lifted and broken. She will spin the Wheel for him and cut him short.

"You are cold," she says to him devoid of emotion.

He is huddled and shivering, pale and drawn in, the ice striking into him, telltale signs of exposure weakening him. He says nothing.

"I have something for you. Something hot," she says and puts the cup on the floor between the bars. "Drink it."

He sits up and goes to it, animal cunning in his eyes.

"You can't keep me in here all day," he says, sweeping his eyes up at the night sky. "In a few hours it'll be light. People will be out walking their dogs on the Common. I'll shout, they'll hear me."

"Drink," she says.

The night is dark and cold and old. In the far distance she can hear the sea on the shore, a gentle breath on the iron stones. No cars move on the front. The city is asleep, huddled in the snow.

He reaches to the cup and puts his hands around it, grateful for its warmth; feels the heat penetrate his body. He sniffs its vapour: a mixture of spices and flavours he cannot identify, but appealing. He gulps a mouthful. Bitter. A sickly, vile bitter taste.

"What the fuck is this?" he says. "It's fucking disgusting."

He throws the cup at her, spilling the liquid on his hand so it burns him. She sidesteps the cup, and it flies back behind her, falling with a hollow crack on the floor.

"Shit!" He rubs his wet hand against his chest. The fluid soaks into his coat, sinking through the layers to the skin beneath.

She straightens, her composure nearly dispelled. She didn't expect this – that he would not drink it. He has swallowed a small amount and there is more on his skin. Will it work? Her mother had said of the potion: "His virtues will be baneful and will corrupt all they touch." But she isn't sure if this touch is what she meant.

She considers the process she was taught. The potion requires an incantation to activate it. The song she knows is an extended, shifting melody line that works on a potion systemically. Will it work topically? She suspects that as things stand, it will require harmonic resonance, where two lines of music cause a deep vibration that calls up deeper magic. She doesn't know if it will work with one singer acting alone

Nevertheless, she prepares to sing. The music of the spheres, the harmonies of the seven planets, will speak to the plants and the powders. The powers governing their virtues will hear and set them to work. She hopes this, but she can't be sure.

She opens her mouth and the notes flood out to create an ancient, unearthly music.

The response in Riley is one of puzzled amusement. His face forms into a sneer as the line goes on.

"What the fuck?" he shouts from the tunnel. *"What the fuck are you doing?"*

There is sadness in her song, and anger. In the tone, a steady unwinding of the grievances she has with the world, an expression of the way she has always existed outside of the world – always different. The melody rises as the words of a forgotten language turn back on themselves and begin again. She sees the patches where the potion has touched him begin to glow, a hint of luminescence that gives off lambent light. He does not see it. All he sees is this crazed Goth girl singing at him and he laughs in her face.

The song comes to an end. The lambency dies. She looks at him, sees no transformation and exhales with bitter disappointment. *It didn't work. Damn it, it didn't work because it was all lies.* The night sky turns above her and lightens a degree in the East. Soon the sky will empty of stars and make way for the day.

It is then that she hears music answering hers. A melody line that echoes her own, but distorts it and provides an underpinning to her tune. It plays again an introductory line, tempting her, calling to her, seducing her to sing again. She feels the urge inside her as the line repeats, an excitement and rising exaltation, and she opens her mouth once more.

This new melody is a harmony, high and elusive, full of laughter and mystery combining with her own. As she sings, the melody it plays fuses with hers. The words and the tune winding together build in power as the resonances grow, the harmonies and dissonances rich and magical, ancient and exotic. It is a measured music, speaking of pain and other worlds and the gentle music of the night. She imagines a world untrammelled with suffering as she sings, a world untouched by the knowledge of life and death. Pure, where the creatures of the world and womankind live without separation. The time before fear entered the garden.

So she sings on.

Riley is staring open-mouthed at something behind her, his face a frozen picture of astonishment and disbelief. She turns to look. On the rampart is a man in red, with red hair and a red goatee beard. Behind him are the upturned horns of the moon, and for a split instant it seems to her that the two points of the horns protrude above the top of his head.

He continues to play, and she considers breaking off the song. It is not that she can't, it is that she doesn't want to, she realises. She must see this spell through. And so, she sings with him, willing the transformation to occur. The glow where the potion touched Riley is brighter now, and Riley notices it. He pats at his clothing as tongues of red, ethereal flame rise up from the cloth, but where his hands touch, they too sprout more flame. The fire spreads across his body and Riley shrieks, somehow the shriek too combining with the melody the singer and violinist play, and magnifying the effect.

Donitza sees him and the blood drains from her face, making it white as the moon, her eyes shadowed and kohl-lined, black and dangerous. He is the outline of a burning man with a black core. She sings on. His shrieks die to a thin nothingness, and as he loses his voice yet more horror and fear fill his face.

Still she sings on, the harmonic shifts, she notes, are growing faster and at times more dissonant. The violinist adds a further twist of his own to her line, changing it even more than before, taking it on a deeper and crueller path than she was ever taught. The melody changes to something brutal that delights in rending and tearing. Donitza tries to lead it back to the clearer line she started with, but finds his line difficult to resist. She feels that she too is caught in a cage, in a coop, while something cruel moves around her. And when she tries to guide the melody line back, the exertion of her will against this harmony creates yet more dissonance. His line, it is so powerful, so alluring. She feels it. Feels it the way addicts do when they promise they will not be controlled by whatever drives them, but always are. She feels it in the way the hollow-eyed men and women on the city's estates feel it when Riley comes to their door. Despite herself, she needs this, needs the affirmation, even though she knows it will do her harm.

So, she succumbs and joins with the Red Man, making a line that is utterly cruel, devoid of heart, brutal in the extreme. It is a relief to her to express this, to make this manifest at last.

Riley is convulsing now. He looks up with horror at the Red Man on the rampart, and Donitza turns and follows his gaze.

Along the walls next to the Red Man countless pairs of eyes appear in the night, green, lambently glowing. The silhouettes of foxes, letting out piercing screeches in a growing crescendo that builds and builds again, and twines with the fierce cruelty in her melody to make a harmony far richer than she had imagined. The tune spills out and amplifies her pain, her loss, her grief – until Eddy, who has been watching the whole mad ritual runs and hides in the workshop, cowering in a corner and stopping his ears with the palms of his hands.

When the spell is wrought, silence descends. There is a second of silent exchange between her and the Red Man. Then with a triumphant look, he salutes her, bows like a seasoned performer, then turns his back. As he does so, she cannot be sure, but she thinks she sees something whip behind him as he goes – a movement as if something follows him. Then he is gone. The foxes on the ramparts are gone, too, their brushes disappearing over the edge. The night is still; the grey light that comes hours before dawn begins to seep into the sky.

She unlocks the gate to the tunnel and steps in. The tunnel stinks of something eldritch and otherworldly, a rich sulphurous stench that claws at her throat and makes her cough. There is a pile of burned clothing on the ground, but Riley is nowhere to be seen.

She kneels and searches among the clothing, eventually seeing a movement underneath the charred cloth. She lifts a blackened scrap to see a homunculus, dark, twisted and ugly squirming there. It stares up at her with blinded eyes and tries to speak, mouthing soundless syllables.

A flicker crosses her face – shock and disgust.

"What have I done?" she asks the echoing walls.

*

Walking back to the workshop, she finally knows she has power. Power she once doubted but that has come back to her like the gulls that are absorbed into the ice in the winter and released again when it thaws. Yes, she has that power – to transform and change and renew. She sees her world open in a way she had not even conceived. "Anything is possible," she tells herself, and feels afraid.

In the workshop, Eddy is cowering on the floor, his head pressed against the wall. He turns his eyes to the woman who stands before him with her severe, kohl-lined face, unsure how to react.

"Stand up," she says, commanding him with a newfound presence. He shuffles to his feet like a schoolboy and casts his face downwards. "Don't worry," she says with a softer voice. "All is fine, Eddy. Thank you. Thank you for your help."

Her warmth for him grows to an impulse. She supposes she loves this simple man whose kindness has in its way helped her connect to her world, a connection that took her back, step by step to her mother's tradition. She looks down on him and takes his face in her hands, kissing him with passionate tenderness on the lips.

When the kiss is over, she looks at him expectantly, awaiting the rush of reciprocation, of the sex urge to manifest itself. He continues to look back at her from the world of eternal surprise on the far side of his glasses.

They stand looking at each other for two seconds more, then he turns.

"I need to fix the village," he says and walks out into the snow, the puzzling moment set aside in his need to set things right.

With a long exhalation she says to the empty workshop: "There never was a prince."

*

For Riley there is a period of blankness. A long cold silence that yawns out like an eternity and then fills with twisted shapes and flames and pain as he floats up toward consciousness.

Eventually, he wakes in the dark; his sense of relief soon dispels in puzzlement and fear.

He is naked, his head feels like a motorway pile-up and he has a blinding migraine. He lies still for a long time, his hands and body resting on a rough-hewn wooden floor. He is shivering in the cold, blinking at blackness.

Despite the throbbing in his head, he calls out. The sound of his voice is absorbed by the walls around him. A dead acoustic. *Where?*

He sits up gingerly, and reaching out finds a coarse blanket on the floor that he snatches and wraps around himself. He gathers his thoughts. The last thing he recalls is Donitza singing. Nothing beyond that but crazy, nightmarish images.

He shouts again, but hears nothing except his own voice dying and experiences a stabbing pain in his head at the exertion. He stands and feels around the room. Coarse walls, thick, striated and fibrous in which he finds an opening. Stepping carefully, he wanders forward and has the sense of a large open area, a vault rising above him. No one is near, he can tell that. Unsure what to do, he sits on the floor and waits.

He stays like this for what might be a few hours, unsure how to mark time. He notices how his body feels different, somehow, stretched and thin, with a hungry centre. Moods pass through him. Anger, frustration, resentment, malice. Then fear comes to him again: that unwelcome visitor that electrifies and weakens. He remembers in a flash a threat of abandonment. Has she followed through? Is this it, here in the darkness? The abandonment she promised?

He frets some more, fixated on this thought until he falls asleep again, dozing fitfully, his dreams filled with more darkness and twisted images.

*

When he wakes, he can hear something moving in the distance. The deep rasp of a heavy surface against another, the bass rumble and shake of something massive moving near him. He tilts his head and tries to make it out.

In the way one can sense one is being watched, he senses something nearby – another consciousness.

"Donitza! Donitza? Are you there?"

He listens to the darkness around him. A low hissing, as of the wind moving in a massive space. Then a movement and a dull thud. He smells something nearby. Food. A rich, meaty smell rising to his nostrils.

He stumbles toward it and finds beneath his hands a roughly hewn table, and an uneven chair. He reaches out in the dark and knocks against something – a vessel of strange design containing something heavy and viscous. It is soup in a bowl, he realises.

He settles to eat it, aware that he is starving. While he eats, he remains aware of that presence, that other consciousness.

"I know you're there," he says to the darkness. "I know it."

No-one replies and after a while longer, when the food is eaten he gropes his way back to the room where he found the blanket.

He is afraid.

*

As winter unfurls into spring, an area of high pressure settles over the city. It is preceded by warm rains that flood down on the town, wiping away its layer of snow that locked the city's sins beneath ice for more than six weeks. An invasion party of pebbledashed snowmen rushing up the beach melts to nothingness, as if a heat ray from a sci-fi movie were turned upon them. The rain clears the streets and people breathe relaxed breaths and smile to the blue sky where birds begin to sing when the high pressure comes.

People unfurl, too. The elderly, who were afraid to step out onto boneshattering smoothness emerge like wrinkled dormice into the light. Children play in the parks; ice-free everyday life begins again. Trips to the shops, journeys to school and to work cease to be logistical exercises. Life moves in the sap of the plants and the currents of the air.

A set of responsibilities has fallen to Donitza. She has hardly seen Celia for weeks, but now she visits and shares a cake with her. When Celia asks where she is staying, Donitza is evasive, smiling over a Chelsea bun and coffee, and changing the subject.

"You look different," Celia says. "Different somehow... Why don't you come back and stay a while with me?"

Donitza responds with gratitude to the warmth of the old woman and wonders how she will say what she wants to say without breaking her heart. She must tell her the truth about her granddaughter. It will give her a chance at last to say goodbye, a wave of the hand to a parting memory. A ghost laid to rest. She wonders if the best thing is to blurt it all out – get the truth before them both. Janey, long gone, will never come back – can she tell her this? – The news arriving on the spring air like a plague wind.

"Celia, I've got something I must tell you – " she begins, but then hesitates. The words about to tumble out mass in her mouth so she can't express them.

Celia frowns and looks afraid. She has recognised the tension in the girl. Her heart is troubled and she waits a while, feeling what her response should be. Then she speaks.

"You know, you never told me about your family."

"My – ?"

"No. Never. I sat and I told you my woes, my troubles. But I realise now that you never told me about yours. But I think," and she says the words lightly as if skating gently over ice, "I think you may not want to."

Donitza feels a tide of uncertainty rising in her, but pushes on.

"Celia, it's about Janey – "

Again she stops, uncertain how to tell this story to soften it enough. Celia stiffens, sitting upright and staring at the girl before her with searching eyes. *She has guessed,* Donitza thinks. *And she doesn't want to know. She doesn't want the pain.* It feels as if time ticks by impossibly slowly. The sun, moving around on its daily course, strikes a finger into the room, and the dust that Celia tries to catch in her duster day after day tumbles and whirls in a galaxy of suspended motes. They both breathe together, both afraid.

"I don't think you want to tell me about your family, do you?" Celia says, on instinct, the words parrying the younger woman's. As if somehow they are duelling – fighting to arrive at a version of the future from their pasts.

"What?"

"But why should you? I have come to think this of the past. Whatever it points to is gone. Don't you think? You can't get it back." She looks down at her tea a moment, slowly pulsing warmth upwards in the air, sunlight striking across the thermal trails casting black tumult on the wall behind. "Since you came to the house, I've been happy," she says and reaches her old hand across the table. "You are like a daughter to me."

Those words stop two trains of time and wind them backwards. Resetting the hands on the eternal clock that marks out people's lives.

"Stay a while."

This is not why Donitza came here. She had sad news to tell. It was, she had believed, her duty. But now..?

She relaxes under the old woman's hand.

"Mama," she says to herself, under her breath, and feels the words and its meaning sink into her psyche as she looks at the older woman.

"Mum."

*

Celia is right when she says Donitza is different now, and in the days after that meeting, the change becomes clearer. Others remark on it. Her musician acquaintances mourn how she does not play any more, others note how she has hennaed her dark hair so it combines with an earthy tone of redness. She seems less drawn, less gaunt than she was, more relaxed, and for the first time in years puts on weight, broadening out her figure. What's more, her eyes are alive as if the spring reaches into her soul and makes her grow.

*

Magic, that apparent breaker of cause and effect has its consequences. Always.

So, the spring comes on, and eventually Donitza realises she must do something about Riley. Stasis is not nature's natural state. It is always flow and continuum.

One afternoon while she is visiting Celia, there is a knock at the door. When Donitza opens it, she sees the same woman police sergeant who came to her before on *that* night. She eyes Donitza closely as she tells her that someone has reported a man called James Peter Riley missing. She explains that he has not answered his mobile, nor responded to tweets. He has disappeared from social media... and the real world, it seems. His phone was last triangulated on the southern side of the island city, weeks before. They are aware that he called by to see her at some point, and they are establishing his movements before his disappearance. Has she heard or seen anything from him?

She denies knowledge of his whereabouts and makes a show of being concerned. Yet when the Sergeant leaves, Donitza has the idea that she doesn't entirely believe her.

The visit prompts her to deal with Riley. She looks back with the luxury of regret on that last night when he came to the fort. She was a fool, she thinks, allowing herself to be ruled by anger and instinct. She has done a terrible thing.

I didn't do it alone, she reminds herself. There is the puzzle of the violinist on the ramparts. Who was he? Her protector? Or The One the Muslims and Christians mention? *The Adversary?* If it were him, what would that mean for her? She thinks of religious people she has heard in the past, who told her that those who dabbled in spell-making would be punished for witchcraft - the nuns in Italy, the boy in Spain, old Radek. She wishes she understood more. Most of all she wishes she could put back the fruits she pulled from the tree; undo the craft she has worked.

She spends her days seeking out ancient knowledge, ordering obscure books from the library and looking up information on the internet. She sleeps at the model village, poring over books as Eddy works on restoring the destruction Riley brought to the place. She sits in meditation and seeks to speak with her mother's shade. But her mother does not come to her.

How can she undo the harm she has done?

Eddy works on. Sometimes, she looks up from her books out of the window as he places a house on the green earth – and she smiles to herself. He is a brother. A connection, just as Celia is a connection, too.

Eddy says little as he works. He sinks back into himself and feels a change coming to himself also. When the sun comes out, he looks up at the sky and feels the urge to bask in the light. He is less and less troubled by the world's size; a sense of freedom seizes him that he has never known before. He thinks less, responding to the world with instinct - and at a deep level has an idea that if it were not for this work holding him here at the Model Village, he would be someone else entirely.

At night he dreams of running through grass and slinking in alleyways, a feral life of secrets and velvet movements. Sometimes he dreams that he makes his way between iron bars down a dark tunnel, and he looks up at a large glass case on a stand. A house. He jumps up, looks in to see a creature there he wants to track down. Feels an instinct to chase the creature around those walls and smother it.

He wakes, sometimes in pain, feeling physically different. He doesn't talk of *that* night – when everything changed. He doesn't tell Donitza how some of the liquid from the cup Riley flung splashed him, and how he has felt the change running through him growing stronger through the days. He is devoted to her as she pores over her books, and is also afraid of her. He will not disturb her.

For Donitza, nothing useful comes from her studies. But in that halcyon time of reflection and learning, she feels the roots that were cut when she was young begin to grow again. She feels a sense of connection with the island clay.

Riley, though she hates to admit it, is another connection. He plays on her mind as she ensures he is fed. She looks at him, this piteous creature and cannot bring herself to tell him what has happened to him. This shrunken husk, this nothing who at least has lost his sight and cannot see his own condition. She feels deeply ashamed at what she did, and has a sense that there will be a reckoning for it. Her mother's warnings and injunctions come to her at these times, ringing in her ears and making her despair.

That is when she is in her more charitable phase, but there are other times when the dark mood takes her and she looks down on him with a sense of loathing as he gropes around the matchstick model of the Guildhall, sightlessly seeking a way out. How pathetic he seems to her, this shrunken, hunched creature who has been the author of so much misery. She laughs to herself about him with a malicious joy that she finds intoxicating and sees him as the wretched king of a cursed domain, sightless and brought low by her. She revels in that thought and sometimes catches herself laughing, shocked at her own cruelty.

When she laughs, sometimes he tries to find the source of his torment. Stumbling out of a low doorway he shouts something toward the sky, shaking his fist. At other times, overwhelmed with fear, he hides and crouches, covering his ears at the mockery he hears. He is a study, she thinks, in the frailty of humanity.

This thought urges her on to further cruelty.

Sometimes, when he is groping his way around his prison, he inexplicably runs up against a door where he was sure there had been none previously. It is ridged, slightly soft and warm to the touch, with three channels running down its length. He pushes against it, angry, confused and then gives up and walks away. Five minutes later the block is gone.

He cannot explain it and cannot know that Donitza, in a moment of impishness, covered the doorway with her hand. He cannot know how she enjoyed feeling him struggle helplessly against her, or how she takes delight in his weakness.

When this phase passes, she is wracked with further guilt and she redoubles her efforts to find a cure. She works on, day and night.

Then, one morning, things begin to change.

The change happens when the owner of the model village arrives to open up the fort after the winter has passed. Neither Eddy nor Donitza are there at the time. They are scrupulous in leaving no trace of themselves when they are absent – a habit Eddy insisted upon. The owner, an older man who runs the model village in his retirement, is looking forward to a day of cleaning and tidying. He dreads to think about the repair work he will have to do. He is convinced vandals will have broken in over the winter and wrecked the place, as they have done time after time over the last few years.

But after he opens the padlocked steel doors and wanders in he is surprised to find the model village in good condition. *It's too good to be true*, he thinks as he stands with arms akimbo wide-stanced in the middle of the courtyard looking at the miniature boats bobbing on the water, the model houses neat and tidy with a fresh lick of paint. "Like the elves and the shoemaker," he says to himself scratching his head, thinking of the story he told his granddaughter from the picture book only a few days before.

By the miniature Post Office he finds, cast to one side, a shawl with tassels, and he wonders whose it is.

When Eddy appears, blinking at the iron gate, he recognises the lad who cleaned for him last season and asks if he knows anything about the amazing condition of the village. Eddy replies with clumsily evasive answers that make the owner smile. Whoever it was, he says to Eddy with a grin, he is grateful.

So, the model village is opened to the public a week early, and the little magic kingdom in the snow, that Eddy and Donitza ruled like sibling monarchs, comes to an end.

The day it does, Eddy vanishes. And when Donitza makes her way back into the fort late in the night in order to take Riley with her, she finds that he, too, has gone.

*

She cannot know what happened earlier that day. She is painfully aware that over the preceding days Riley's mind had grown progressively weaker, a madness breaking in upon him in his sightless loneliness. Images of the past haunted his blind vision. The impossibility of the violinist on the ramparts. The Red Man with the moon as horns. She doesn't know that he had started to wonder if perhaps he had died and was now in hell. Or how at other times he talked to the walls and wept for himself and his lonely condition, wishing he were dead.

Nor does she know that some of her restorative spell-casting had at last started to work. How that day he had woken to find the room he slept in filled with light. In excitement he looked at his hands before his face, and though they were blurred and vague, they were definitely shapes he knew. He found his way through the passages he had learned so well and, finding a turning he had missed before, stumbled down queerly-crafted steps out of the building. He saw ahead of him the vague outline of a corridor leading away into a massive distance. A gigantic space, as if he were looking at the great arch of an enormous cathedral, the likes of which he had never seen.

She does not know how he ran toward it, elated and afraid. His eyesight was still unclear and dim, but he ran toward the light, stopping with a jarring jolt, falling to the floor as he hit a wall of glass.

She has no idea how he lay there, stunned for a while, then turned back and looked up at his prison, agog. Rearing above him, the matchstick model of the Guildhall, where he had been trapped for weeks.

Nor does she know how, at that very moment, a pair of fascinated eyes on the far side of the glass saw him, and with the determination of childhood, reached into the case with a massive fleshy palm and snatched him up. None of this she knows. Nor how the boy told his mother what he had found, and she, in the way that mothers do, told him not to be so stupid; or how Riley was crammed, struggling, into a pocket to be inspected later.

*

You may see Donitza, one day, walking across the Common on a sunkissed spring afternoon, a day filled with light so freshly bright and hard that the trees look as if their shadows have been drawn with the fine head of a draughtsman's pen. The city these days is her home, and *home* means something to her in the way it means to most of us wherever we are. Its meaning is ambivalent. A place not only of happiness but also of pain all wrapped up at once in the great inseparable flux of events.

If you see her on such a bright day, you will see that she is thoughtful, perhaps remembering a day from her past, not many weeks after she moved back in with Celia.

She often thinks of that day because it is still a puzzle to her. She remembers she had a camouflage bag over her shoulder and a passport in her pocket and was heading on a goodbye walk that would take her from the Common, along the seafront eventually to the bus depot by the railway station, where her ticket to leave was booked.

She had changed in the weeks that had passed since she moved back in with Celia. Broadened some more, as if the tight control she exerted in her life had begun to relax itself and the very edges of her being were responding.

As she walked by the war memorial, not far from the place a giant ship's anchor squatted on a dais, a car pulled up beside her. An old classic of some sort – a retro rod that you sometimes see going along the seafront – all black vintage angles, chrome and tail fins, with a line of flames painted along the car's lower half, like a cauldron on a camp fire.

"Hello," said a voice she recognised.

Lambent green eyes were looking out from the left-hand driver's seat. A mischievous smile above a red goatee.

"Get in," he said. "I'll give you a lift."

She couldn't resist her curiosity. Sinking into the soft leather seats she bored accusatory eyes into him.

"Who are you?" she blurted as he ticked the indicator and the car pulled away with impossible smoothness, a purring engine that spoke of hidden power.

"Did your mother never tell you not to get into cars with strangers?" he answered with a flat tone, half joyous, half unsettling.

Before she could answer, he said:

"Tell me, how are you feeling?" The tone he used was like the counsellor's concern for his client. "Are you over your loss?"

Donitza looked out at the squat tower of the western pier, a fantasy of 1960s design, and nodded to herself. "I used to think that my mother broke the magic circle we had spent so many years inhabiting together when she helped someone who came to her door. But now I understand she had to help him, because she was connected to him. Connected to him because he was on this earth too, and we are all flesh together."

"Ah, helping others," Lissitch said with a tone she couldn't read. "There is nothing like it."

They were heading toward a roundabout. Lissitch took the car smoothly left and they motored along by a Gothic confection of redbrick towers.

"And now what do you think?" he asked.

She took a few breaths.

"That she was right. She was connected, and it is a shame to lose a connection. I am losing one. Celia is old and confused. She needs help. And I have lost others I was connected to. I don't know where they are."

"Yet you are leaving."

She nodded. "There is something I must do. There are trials in my home country. I will make my deposition, give my statement. See justice served. Then I will come back."

He took the car up past an old military gate and a shopping centre beyond, the place where once an Empire armed its war machine, now given over to shopping and food. She looked at him once more, unable to get the question out of her mind that had gnawed her for weeks.

"That night. You helped me cast a spell. An evil, evil spell. There were packages on the ground that my mother had made for me when I was a girl – they came from the violin case. But I don't think all of them did. Some of them were left by you. The ones that enabled the darker spells. My mother always said they were forbidden to me..."

"I couldn't say," he shrugged. "You had a choice to use them."

She brushed the argument aside:

"You led the melody. You made something cruel even crueller. Who are you? What did you make me do?"

His eyes flamed then and he laughed loudly – an unsettling sound that reminded her of both the sunlight on the sea and the danger in its depths.

"Perhaps you imagined it was me," he answered. "All I can tell you is I am a counsellor. I help people find themselves. Nothing you have done was not inside of you already."

"You tricked me!" she insisted. "You took me down a path I would never have taken otherwise."

He frowned, a shadow crossing his face that made her afraid.

"I think those days are gone, for you," he said, with an aggressive tone. "Of claiming innocence. Of blaming others for your own choices."

Then, as quickly as it came, the shadow passed. "Will you play the violin again?"

"No," she said. "I will paint. Perhaps one day, after I have said goodbye to Celia, I will sing."

"I told you, I am a violinist," he said with unexpected force. "I can get your violin fixed!" Then he relaxed and said lightly, "Think how your friends admire you when you play. Surely, you are tempted to lift the bow again?"

She considered him a while, a powerful instinct that she would do well to go her own way from him.

"I wouldn't want to unlock that craft again," she said. "That time has gone."

"A shame," he said. "You have great skill."

He pulled the car to a halt near the bus depot. She was early and the bus that would take her to the airport had not yet arrived.

"I should go," she said, clicking open the door. "Goodbye."

"Very well," he smiled again, a hard expression crossing his face as she stepped out and closed the door. He pressed a button and lowered the window, saying to her. "This town is not such a bad place to bring up a girl."

She gasped and looked down at her stomach, laying a defensive palm across it. Did it show already? Surely not. Yet here it was – another connection to the town.

"It *will* be a girl," he said in a flat voice, to her confusion. "And what of the father?"

Her shoulders fell forward and she leaned in to look at him, vulnerable. A sickness lurched through her and she found herself wracked with emotions. Guilt, confusion, frustration.

"I don't know," she finally said.

Lissitch nodded to himself and seemed satisfied. "As it should be," he said. "But think: if you were to see him again, how would you protect yourself? And how would you protect your girl? You have the potential to wield great power over the people here. To make life comfortable for you and your family."

He smiled as she blinked at his words; she was swayed perhaps a little by the prospect they offered. But then, she had to consider that there was this man: Lissitch. What did *he* want? A recruit? An ally? A slave?

Perhaps he sensed the thoughts in her head, the instinctive distrust of him. Before she could ask him, he spoke again:

"You know he called you a witch. He was right. You can't stop being one."

With an expression perhaps of impatience, he pushed the gear stick home and drove off, his hand making a high slow gesture of goodbye as he receded along the road.

*

Thus her remembrances of the last time Donitza saw Reynold Lissitch fifteen months before. She often revisits them to seek a clue about him. She is doing so again as she walks across the Common, having stolen a few minutes to enjoy the sunshine. She heads home, up through the tight Victorian streets to Celia's house. It is her home, now.

The sunlight shines brightly into the house as she opens the door. She sees a young woman holding Donitza's baby, silhouetted in the light flooding in from the kitchen.

Vee, a friend she made in ante-natal classes. A single woman who lives just nearby whom Donitza found has so much in common with her. She also lost someone and fell pregnant at around the same time as herself. Donitza has not revealed that she also knew Riley.

"Hello, good walk?" Vee says, glancing up with a smile, looking healthier and happier than she has in a long time.

"Very good," Donitza answers, then sees a mess of tangled fur, the remains of a mouse dropped on the carpet before her, as if placed there as an offering.

"What's this? Not again?"

"Afraid so," Vee answers. "But we've found the culprit at last."

"No? Who?" Donitza asks, surprised.

As she speaks, a cat slinks in from the garden. A stray that has decided to attach itself to the household, seeming to have come from nowhere. She notices the way it walks, as if its legs are sprung and its feet never quite fully touch the ground.

"Is this him?" Donitza asks.

She kneels and reaches out her hand. It comes to her and rubs against her fingers.

"What a funny little thing. So odd looking."

The expression on its face makes her laugh.

Its eyes are wide and round, with lines above them in high semi circles. *Such a strange effect*, she thinks.

As if he is wearing glasses, and the whole world and everything that happens on the other side of them is a never-ending source of surprise.

Epilogue

"I READ it in a book," says Jord with a smile to his brother, Daryl. "They used to do it in Ancient Rome."

They are sitting in their bedroom, gazing with hostile eyes at the figure Daryl has pulled from his pocket. Jord looks at him with sudden fear on his face.

"Is it really him, though?" he says, with remembered terror. "I mean, come on, how can it be?"

The other shrugs and then gives a thoughtful grin.

"I don't know," he says. "I mean, what about aliens? It could be aliens, right, who have this shrink ray, and they come down – and ba-sham – vooop – it hits you and you shrink down, like really tiny."

He does the sound effect with surprising energy, shaking the naked figure of Riley that he is holding in his hands. Riley tries to shout, but he finds his voice is weak.

"Is this hell?" Riley asks himself. "Is this what hell is like? The Devil on the ramparts, and now this?"

The boys see his angry movement.

"Look, he's trying to say something," Jord says.

Daryl comes close, putting his mouth beside Riley's head. "What is it? What do you want?"

Riley tries to shout again, but he realises they can't hear him. His voice is like the buzzing of a fly to them. Daryl shakes him, up and down in the air.

"Put him in the ball," says Jord, decisively. "Go on!" He holds the parts of the hamster ball around Daryl's hands, and the fat, scrub-faced boy drops him in.

"There."

Riley makes a run for it, flailing like a kid in one of the plastic airballs they sometimes have on the lake in the summer that the kids flop around in. The ball wobbles away for cover. Daryl punts it with a toe so it rolls up against the wall.

"Goal!" he shouts, waving his arms in the air.

"Little shits," Riley shouts, when he recovers, waving his fist at them. This isn't hell, he's decided. And even if it is, the habit of domination and bullying reasserts itself. His voice is echoed and amplified in the ball and the two boys hear him. "You fucking little shits, you wait till I get back to normal!"

The boys look at each other, afraid.

"It's him. It *is* him!" Daryl screams. "Oh, bloody hell. I didn't think it could be him, but it bloody well is!"

Jord takes hold of the ball and holds it level with his face. He eyes the man inside, smaller than his fist, naked – but undeniably Riley.

"What do we do with him?" Daryl says.

"I dunno... Do what we said?"

They look at each other and nod agreement.

Daryl adds: "Like they did in Ancient Rome?"

"Yes," says Jord, resolution on his face. "Just like they did back then."

They unscrew the ball and pull the struggling man-figure from it. Then they go over to the corner of the room, by the window. There's the secondhand cage, shining in the sunlight, the little water bottle attached to one side.

With a deft movement they open the door and drop him in, on to a bed of shavings.

"Let me out. Let me out!" Riley shouts up, through the bars. The two boys are looming over him, their faces fixed intently on him, a look of fascination at what is about to happen.

It's then that Riley hears the noise behind him. The sound of an animal awakened by his voice, snuffling. A face appears from the pile of shavings. A gigantic, whiskered face. Riley turns and backs away from the creature.

The animal sniffs him again.

Somewhere in its rodent brain it remembers this smell and in the dull way that connections are made, makes an association.

The boys look on. Such sport. They've never had so much fun.

END

*

A Note from the Author.

Thanks for choosing to read my novel. I do hope you liked it. Working as an independent author can be tough, so if you enjoyed The Snow Witch, please tell people about her. Writing a review or giving a rating on Amazon.co.uk and/or Goodreads.com would really help. You might also mention Donitza on your blog (if you have one), on social media or recommend her story to friends.

Finally, thank you again. Without you, I wouldn't write.

3 books of original fiction you might enjoy...

Day of the Dead
by Matt Wingett, William Sutton, Diana Bretherick and other members of Portsmouth Writers Hub

Let's talk about Death.

After all, it's the one thing we all have in common. Eventually. Let's explore it, cry about it, tremble at it, laugh with it.

Then let's write stories about Death...

Twenty authors have done exactly that, giving you twenty-eight tales about the one subject no-one wants to talk about, but everyone knows will come to them.

Whether it's a puzzling pronouncement about how to handle humans in another world, a story of a man who does not know he is dead, the true story of saying goodbye to Dad, or making lipsmacking use of a departed friend, this collection explores Death in its many different guises, offering up twenty-eight brilliant takes on mortality, from the spine-tingling, scary and screwy to the strange, touching and poignant.

Often wry, sometimes creepy, always surprising, the stories in this book were drawn through the massive pool of talent connected with Portsmouth Writers' Hub, and boasts internationally-published authors as well as talented newcomers to the printed page.

The authors of the Day of the Dead invite you to join their celebration of all things mortal.

Enjoy...

Dark City – Portsmouth Tales of Haunting and Horror
by William Sutton, Diana Bretherick and others

Join 18 masters of the macabre, the strange, and the bizarre as they journey into a dark and richly reimagined Portsmouth that you will never forget. Here you can meet a man who finds himself transforming into the Tricorn Centre. Discover the mysterious pulse that beats beneath the pavement of this living city that craves blood and sacrifice. Witness damnation in a hellish vision of Victorian Portsmouth, and learn just how difficult it can be getting two severed heads through customs at the port. Like the waves that lap the fringes of this waterfront city, past and present flow back and forth in these tales of haunting and horror, dragging ghosts and their tragedies in their wake.

Portsmouth Fairy Tales for Grown-Ups
by Matt Wingett, William Sutton, Diana Bretherick, Tessa Ditner and other Portsmouth writers.

25 Stories, 11 writers, 1 city.

This collection of fairy tales for grown-ups contains dark moral tales, historical fiction, sci-fi, comedy, fantasy, crime, memoir and surreal fiction. All the stories have been freshly-written and all are set in and around the UK's only island city.

No chocolate box visions or soppy princesses in sight, the writers have used this magical genre to explore grown-up dilemmas, such as money problems, fear of rivalry in a relationship, floods, memories and changing bodies.

Find out why the real Guildhall clock is buried in an underground city to save time. Hear about the man who wished himself onto a ship in a whisky bottle. Discover why a Victorian detective joined forces with the circus to fight Spice Island's criminals. Embrace your bank statement or the ghost ship will get you.

Some stories delve into the city's rich island geography, others focus on rural Hampshire, its cow pats, mushrooms and breweries. Some have taken their favourite urban location and woven it into fantastical narratives that stretch back to Victorian times, or forward to a dystopian future.

Raw, mischievous, dark and yet familiar, these tales showcase a city bubbling with literary minds.

Non Fiction

Conan Doyle and the Mysterious World of Light
by Matt Wingett

*Why did the man who created Sherlock Holmes
also believe in ghosts?*

From early in his medical career, Arthur Conan Doyle was fascinated by the paranormal. In 1887 – the year his first Sherlock Holmes novel was published – he became convinced of the existence of spirits.

Even as the fame of his ultra-rational creation grew, Doyle investigated poltergeists, spirit photography and much more.

Then, as the deaths of the Great War mounted, he announced to a shocked world that Spiritualism was a "New Revelation".

Yet, still he continued writing Sherlock Holmes stories. How could this apparent contradiction exist in one man's mind?

Drawing on Conan Doyle's original articles and letters for the Spiritualist magazine *Light*, you will meet the men and women who supported, agreed and argued with him, including the Press, the Church, scientists and writers.

Conan Doyle and the Mysterious World of Light is volume one of a three part series tracing Doyle's Spiritualism to his death in 1930. This fascinating volume also includes every article and letter Doyle wrote for *Light* between 1887 and 1920 - many of which have never been previously published in book form.

Order at Life Is Amazing - www.lifeisamazing.co.uk

Lightning Source UK Ltd.
Milton Keynes UK
UKHW052150140919
349739UK00019B/902/P